CW00863993

LOTTIE'S RUN

DAVID WAUGH

CONSTANCE BOOKS

ISBN 978-190964-455-7
Printed and bound in Great Britain.
Published by Constance Books
Produced by YouCaxton Publications

Contents

DAVID WAUGH

David Waugh is Senior Teaching Fellow at Durham University where he is also the subject leader for Primary English. He has published extensively in Primary English. David is a former deputy headteacher and was Regional Adviser for ITT for the National Strategies from 2008 to 2010. He began writing children's stories for his grandchildren and has published extracts in some of his books on Primary English, as well as in an interactive DVD: *Developing Literacy in Initial Teacher Training.*

David is married to Rosemary and has two children and three grandchildren.

ACKNOWLEDGEMENTS

This story was written during a holiday in France as a bedtime story for my granddaughters Kate and Alex Downing. Their response encouraged me to write every afternoon for a fortnight and their comments helped shape the tale. I am very grateful to them.

I am also extremely grateful to my student, Laura Ryan, and to the children of Green Gates Primary School, Redcar and their teacher, Dinah Andrews, who responded with such enthusiasm when I read *Lottie's Run* to them that I decided to publish it. The two mornings I spent with them were among the most uplifting in my forty-year teaching career.

I am grateful to Stuart Trotter, whose illustrations can be found in such esteemed works as Rupert Annuals, for his superb illustrations for my story.

Finally, I am indebted to my wife, Rosemary, for her proof-reading and for her suggestions and improvements to the story.

CHAPTER ONE

IN THE WOODS

Darkness enveloped her like a blanket. The smells of night time woods filled her nostrils: damp grass, sweet and musty leafmould. Above her, the branches of hundreds of trees creaked and swayed in the light breeze. There were other noises too. Small scurrying sounds as woodland creatures sought food or shelter. Lottie thought many of them were keeping an eye out for the owls she had heard hooting a few moments earlier. Daytime woods were friendly, inviting places to play and hide in. She had never realised that they changed character at night.

But it wasn't the woodland creatures or the darkness which Lottie feared the most as she snuggled into the moist bracken which she hoped would hide her. It was the three people who were out there somewhere looking for her. She knew they couldn't be far away, and she listened for footsteps, breaking twigs and alarm calls from birds. When a nightjar screeched as it flew through a nearby clearing, she caught her breath and felt the pain of fear deep in her stomach. Then there was a rustling in the undergrowth behind her and she turned as quietly as she could, terrified that it might be the kidnappers, to find herself staring through the darkness at three roe deer.

They stood, alert and still, checking for their own safety, unaware that she was watching them. Despite her predicament, despite her pounding heart and dry mouth, she was entranced by their beauty. Like her, they were constantly afraid of being captured or killed, but, unlike her, they knew the woods and the places to hide from hunters and other predators. If they had to run, they would know where to run to: if Lottie had to run she would have to blunder her way through brambles, overhanging branches and thick undergrowth.

Suddenly, the deer pricked up their ears and, as one, galloped away from the clearing. Lottie looked around to see what had startled them and saw, perhaps fifty metres away, the silhouettes of two men. She had to make a decision: run like the deer or stay in her hiding place and hope they didn't find her.

CHAPTER TWO
CAPTURE

It was less than ten hours since Lottie's world had been turned upside down. One minute she was happily coming out of school, her brown eyes beaming, knowing she'd be going to Lauren's party the next night; knowing she'd be going to see her father playing football for England in the afternoon; knowing she and her friend, Ellie, would be having a take away and an evening in front of the telly at Ellie's house that night. Her mum was going to take her sister, Rachel, to a film and then pick Lottie up at lunchtime the next day. Her dad was staying in the hotel with his team mates. Then it had happened. She still couldn't believe she'd been so stupid.

She'd come out of school still wearing her games kit; a maroon hoody, navy blue polo shirt, black shorts and trainers, with her clothes stuffed into her bag and her dark curly hair loose and messy after playing rounders. Ellie had been to the dentist and her mum had arranged for her friend, Sarah, to pick Lottie up. She had looked for Sarah's car. The car was there, but it wasn't Sarah who had opened the rear door for her.

Instead, a smily, dark-haired young woman had said, "Hi Lottie, Sarah's really sorry but she can't pick you up today and she's asked me to collect you instead. She told me to give you this to make up for it." The woman had held out a large dark chocolate Magnum ice lolly, Lottie's favourite, which was really welcome after a day which had ended with a games lesson. Lottie had climbed into the car and taken the ice cream. How stupid could she be? Her mother had told her never to go with strangers. Her teachers had told her never to go with strangers. For goodness sake, the whole class had designed "Never Go with Strangers" posters only two weeks ago. But still she had climbed into the car.

It took about three minutes for her to realise her mistake. The car had pulled up at the side of the road as soon as it had left the village, and two men had climbed in. Before she knew what was happening, they had put a handkerchief over her mouth and she had become instantly sleepy.

The next thing she knew was a feeling of being shaken. She was in the dark and someone was shaking her. Her ankles hurt. She moved to rub them and found that her hands wouldn't move: they were caught in something – no, they were tied together. Her hands were tied and so were her ankles; that was why they hurt. And the shaking was going on and on. Someone was speaking too; a voice close to her saying, "Lottie! Lottie!" The voice was rather muffled, but she could tell it belonged to a woman and she could hear other voices further away. The darkness must be a blindfold; something thick and dark was around her head.

"Lottie! Wake up, Lottie!" Could she go on pretending to be asleep? They must have seen her move though. Who were these people? Where had they taken her, and why? She heard another voice, a man's, saying something about a mobile phone: "... mobile number. Tell us your father's mobile number!"

At first she couldn't speak. She was terrified. But gradually she realised that she had to do something if she was to have any chance of being free again.

"Who are you? What do you want?" she asked, still not sure whom she was talking to.

"Listen Lottie!" said the female voice. It sounded familiar and she recognised it as belonging to the woman who had met her from school, "Just do what we tell you and everything will be all right. Tell us your father's mobile number and we might be nice to you."

Lottie hesitated. Why did they want to know? Did they want to harm her father? If they wanted to harm her, why would they want to contact her father? She decided it would be best to try to be helpful, but she wanted something in return.

"If I tell you, will you take this blindfold off me, please?"

A male voice replied, and Lottie was sure that the person was not English. "I regret, ma'm'selle, it is not possible that we do that. It is of the importance most great that you are not seeing our faces."

"Well in that case, I'm afraid I can't help you," said Lottie with a voice which sounded much braver than she felt. She heard another, deeper male voice.

"OK, it is necessary that you must listen most carefully, for I shall explain one time only. You can do nothing: you can ask us for nothing. We have the guns and you must do as we ask. The escape is not possible. Now, the number of the phone of your father or it will go most bad for you."

Lottie knew when to give in: "07836 595800," she said, "but please tell me what you want with me."

"We don't want to hurt you." It was the woman's voice again. She spoke with an accent Lottie was used to, not like the men who Lottie thought must be from another country: France maybe?

"We are needing to talk to your father. We are needing him to do something for us."

"Why not just ask him?"

"If he is knowing that you are with us, he is more likely to agree. He wouldn't want anything to be happening to you, would he?"

"What kind of thing?" Lottie felt really scared now.

The woman's voice sounded a little kinder: "If your father agrees to help us, then nothing at all. If he is sensible, then you will be going home safe and sound."

"What if he doesn't agree?"

"Well in that case..." Then one of the male voices broke in over the woman's gentler tones.

"You better hope he does agree quick, because if he do not, then the future for you do not look very good at all!"

CHAPTER THREE

LOTTIE'S FAMILY

Her father was different. All he had ever wanted to do was become a famous footballer and he had more than achieved his ambition. Steve Parry had been captain of England for the last three years and his picture was seen on billboards and in newspapers all over the country. Lottie could hardly turn on the television without seeing her father advertising something. She'd lost count of the things he'd promoted, but knew they included razors, deodorant, breakfast cereals, yoghurt and at least one make of car which he had told Lottie he wouldn't be seen dead in.

All of this advertising, as well as his football, meant that Lottie's dad was famous: very famous indeed. So famous that people seemed to follow him almost wherever he went. They couldn't go shopping like a normal family, because people just wouldn't leave him alone. They wanted to ask him about the last match or the next match, and they wanted his autograph or a photograph of them smiling alongside him. "Why don't you just tell them you're busy?"

her mum had said once, and he'd explained to all of them why he never turned anyone away, no matter how bad their timing.

"When I was twelve I waited for two hours with my mate in the pouring rain outside United's ground to collect autographs, and when the players finally came out, do you know how many of them stopped to sign our autograph books?" Lottie's father answered his own question, "One, that's how many, and he wasn't even in the team!"

"The rotten so-and-so's!" said her mum.

"Exactly! I'd waited all that time in the rain and all they had to do was write their names in a book. They went off and climbed into their flashy cars that they could only afford because people like me paid to watch them play, and they left us standing there dripping wet. I never went to see United again and when I was sixteen I joined Rovers, even though United offered me more money."

"Good for you, Dad!" said Lottie and gave him a hug.

"Thanks, love. So you can see why I never refuse anyone an autograph or a picture if they ask for one, and why I always ask their names and write a message, even if it's only, "With best wishes to Mark from Steve Parry". If they're anything like me, they treasure those things and they tell their friends and people start to think that perhaps footballers aren't all overpaid spoilt brats."

Lottie's mum had remained quiet while Steve spoke, but she caught his eye. "But sometimes your good nature backfires on you, doesn't it Steve?"

There was a silence. Rachel, who had only been two at the time, was the only one who wasn't aware of the awful time they'd all had the previous year after Steve was pictured on the front page of the News of the Globe kissing, or rather being kissed by, a blonde lady in a night club. There had been more pictures inside the paper of them leaving the nightclub and getting into a taxi together. Then there was a story, based on the woman's evidence, about them going back to her flat. Lottie vividly remembered the journalists and photographers camped outside their house, surrounding the car whenever they went in or out of the drive.

Her dad had told them it was all untrue and that he was going to sue the Globe to prove it, but for two weeks life had been a nightmare for the family. Lottie had insisted on going to school, despite being told she could stay at home or with her grandparents, but although most people never mentioned the story, Emma Hardy had cut out some of the articles and passed them round, until Mrs Jones, the Headteacher, had confiscated them and told the class that the subject was not to be mentioned again.

Two weeks later, the Globe printed a front page article headed, "Sorry Steve – we were wrong!" in

News of the

Sunday, 26th January, 2014

Sorry Steve - we were wrong!

The Globe wishes to apologise unreservedly for an article published in a recent edition in which we mistakenly suggested that England football captain, Steve Parry had been conducting a secret relationship with Miss Rene Billington.

Further investigations have revealed that this was entirely untrue and the Mr Parry remains a loyal and loving husband and father.

Ren
foll
imp

The
that
rela
the
beh

which it admitted that it had discovered that Steve had not gone to the woman's flat, and that he had helped her into taxi and paid for it because she was too drunk to walk, and he thought she might have an accident. The taxi driver had contacted the paper and told them this, and the woman had finally admitted that she had lied and that she had kissed Steve rather than the other way round, because she had told him she wanted a picture to show her mum.

The newspaper agreed to pay Steve one million pounds to avoid being taken to court, and he had promised to donate all of it to the charity Becky worked for, which helped provide special equipment for hospitals to help babies who were born prematurely.

Steve and Becky had supported the charity since Rachel was born and would have died if the special apparatus hadn't been available at the hospital.

The week after Steve made the donation, another Sunday newspaper printed an article headed, "A National Treasure", which Lottie had framed and hung on her bedroom wall (although she took it down occasionally if she and her father had a row!).

A National Treasure

Three weeks ago a rival newspaper printed a badly-researched and wholly inaccurate story about one of the finest footballers this country has ever produced. As a result, his family was put under severe strain and the player was brought close to breaking point. We condemn this kind of journalism totally.

Steve Parry has shown himself not only to be completely innocent of the Globe's accusations, but also to be a true gentleman and a very special human being. How many of today's overpaid footballers would have passed up the opportunity to add another million to their bank balances? Not many, we'd wager. But Steve Parry handed over every penny of the money, which the Globe so rightly paid as compensation for their dreadful error of judgement, to a charity which he and his wife have long supported.

Steve Parry has come up the hard way. He was married at seventeen and he and his wife have brought

The Daily

Sunday, January 26th, 2014

A National Treasure

Three weeks ago a rival newspaper printed a badly-researched and wholly inaccurate story about one of the finest footballers this country has ever produced. As a result, his family was put under severe strain and the player was brought close to breaking point. We condemn this kind of journalism totally.

Steve Parry has shown himself not only to be completely innocent of the Globe's accusations, but also to be a true gentleman and a very special human being. How many of today's overpaid footballers would have passed up the opportunity to add another million to their bank balances? Not many, we'd wager. But Steve Parry handed over every penny of the money, which the Globe so rightly paid as compensation for their dreadful error of judgement, to a charity which he and his wife have long supported.

Steve Parry has come up the hard way. He was married at seventeen and he and his wife have brought up their family in the right way, when lesser folk might have avoided their responsibilities. His te

Ren foll imp

The that rela the beh of a exp in li its beh con or v

It m tota thin dec mos

up their family in the right way, when lesser folk might have avoided their responsibilities. His terrific work ethic and professionalism, added to his natural footballing talent, have made him the best England captain for years. He's well known for never refusing an autograph hunter, no matter how inconvenient, and he probably performed the most sporting act ever seen in an international match when he deliberately missed a penalty against France last season. He is widely admired and rightly so, and deserves better than to be lied about in a Sunday newspaper.

In short, Steve Parry is a national treasure of whom we should all be proud.

Lottie knew the article off by heart and swelled with pride every time she read it or even thought about it. Steve had suggested she take it down from her wall, but was secretly pleased that she didn't. And Becky had read the article, given Steve a hug and said, "National Treasure, eh? They might not call him that if they had to live with him! They might want to make him into buried treasure instead!"

And they'd all laughed, as they so often did in the Parry household.

CHAPTER FOUR

PRISONER

"Put it on the speaker phone," Lottie heard one of the men say. There was a pause as she heard numbers being tapped into a mobile phone. There was ringing and then her father's voice: "Hi, who's calling?"

They had put tape over Lottie's mouth and she had been told that they would take it off to let her speak to her father, but if she didn't do as she was told they'd put it back on and leave it on.

The woman spoke. "Is that Steve Parry?"

"Depends who's calling. You're not a journalist are you?" Lottie could almost tell that her father would be smiling as he said this.

"I'm afraid not, Mr Parry. I want you to listen very carefully. Don't hang up. Your daughter's life is at stake!"

"What do you mean? Do you mean Lottie or Rachel? Who are you?" Lottie felt the panic in her father's voice.

"We have Lottie here with us, Mr Parry. In a moment, she's going to speak to you and then we're going to tell you what you need to do if you ever want to see her again."

In the stunned silence which followed, the tape was ripped sharply from Lottie's mouth causing her to gasp with pain. "Speak to your father, Lottie. Tell him we mean business," said the woman firmly.

Lottie took a deep breath. "Dad, are you there?"

"Course I am, love, are you all right. Have they hurt you, because if they do..."

"Listen dad, please! I'm OK, but I'm frightened. They've tied me up and blindfolded me. There's three of them..." A hand went over her mouth sharply. "That's enough!" said one of the men. "Put the tape over her mouth and lock her in the back room."

As she was dragged struggling from the room, Lottie heard a painful cry from her father. "Lottie!" he called, "Lottie, don't worry, I'll find you. You'll be all right..."

A door was locked behind her and she beat her fists on it and made muffled, anguished noises, but no-one took any notice. She gave up and strained to hear the telephone conversation. She'd never heard such anger in her father's voice before, but eventually he listened as the woman told him what he had to do if he wanted to his daughter again.

In the match the next day, England were playing Andorra, a tiny country whose team hardly ever scored a goal let alone won. England should win easily, probably by five or six goals to nil, but the men wanted Steve to make sure that Andorra scored twice. He would have to make deliberate mistakes if they were to do that, but if he didn't, he'd never see Lottie again.

When Steve objected, the men reminded him that he'd deliberately missed a penalty in the match against France last year, so they were sure this would be no problem. They told him that if he told anyone about the deal, even his wife, they'd kill Lottie and it would be his fault.

Lottie hardly heard her father say a word during the conversation, but at the end he'd said he would do as they asked, but that if they harmed a single hair of her head he'd follow them to the ends of the earth and see that they got what they deserved.

"Just do as you are told, monsieur, and all will be well. Keep your phone switched on, we'll talk to you later!"

Behind the locked door, Lottie felt anger rise as she thought about what the gang wanted her father to do. She knew enough about football to know that the gang had probably bet a lot of money on Andorra scoring twice and that, as this would normally be highly unlikely, they probably stood to win a lot of cash. She was furious that they'd mentioned her dad's missed penalty in the same breath as their nasty scheme. That had been very different. He'd almost become a hero because of it and he'd received a special medal for sportsmanship.

She remembered watching the match on television and seeing endless replays of the incident. The French goalkeeper had collided with the goalpost and his head had almost immediately been covered with blood. One of his team mates had picked the ball up to stop the game, but after the goalkeeper had been treated and replaced by a substitute, the referee had awarded a penalty to England. The French players had been furious and had surrounded the referee to protest, but Steve had pulled the captain to one side and spoken quietly to him, and the captain had called his players to him and they had stood aside as Steve picked up the ball, carried it to where his own players were gathered, and spoke to them.

The replays showed that there had been some arguing, but that Steve had pointed and spoken firmly to the team. He then walked over to the penalty spot, placed the ball carefully, took a step back and kicked the ball towards the goal so gently that the goalkeeper had to step forward to pick it up.

The French crowd were at first mystified, but then realised what had happened and broke into thunderous applause for the sporting Englishman. The next day's newspapers in England, France and around the world were full of praise for England, and particularly Steve, for showing that sportsmanship was not dead. He was already well on his way to becoming a national treasure.

Now Lottie thought of him having to make deliberate mistakes again, but not because an opponent was injured or because it was the sporting

thing to do. He had to make mistakes to help crooks to make money. And, of course, she thought with a shiver, to save her life.

CHAPTER FIVE
ESCAPE

Lottie decided she would gain nothing by panicking, banging on the door, or wasting her energy in other ways. She needed to think.

Unable to see because of the blindfold or move very much because her wrists and ankles were bound, she had few distractions. She thought about escape and quickly came to the conclusion that it would be impossible, unless they freed her arms and legs and took away the blindfold. She felt around her and found what seemed to be a bed. Despite the restraints, she managed to climb onto it and tried to make herself as comfortable as possible. It smelt musty and damp, as if no-one had slept in it for a while.

Lottie had always done her best thinking in bed. Her dad had told her that he liked to make pictures in his head of things he'd do on the football pitch and then go and try them in the next match. She tried to picture an escape, but without even knowing what the building she was in looked like or where it was, this simply didn't work. Then she had an idea.

They had gagged her with tape; tape which came off

easily, if painfully, when they pulled it. She wondered if her blindfold was also tape. If it was, she might be able to get it off. She moved around on the bed until she felt her face touch something hard, which she assumed must be a wooden bed head. She rubbed her cheek against it until she felt something pulling against her skin. It was tape. She rubbed again and felt the tape pull away from her skin a little. This hurt. She'd always been told that pulling off a plaster quickly hurt far less than doing it bit by bit, and now she knew this was true of whatever tape the kidnappers had used too.

Gradually, excruciatingly painfully, Lottie began to remove the tape until suddenly there was light. The light was fuzzy, but it was definitely there. They'd put something over her eyes before applying the tape and she thought it must be cotton wool. With a few more minutes of rubbing her face against the bed head, Lottie managed to pull the tape away enough for the cotton wool to fall from one eye when she shook her head. She blinked wildly. Even in a gloomy room, the light hurt her eye after being blindfold. Lottie looked around her.

The room was sparsely furnished, with a wardrobe, a chest of drawers, a wooden chair and the single bed on which she lay. There was a window, but the curtains were drawn. She needed to see what lay outside the window to know where she was and to consider whether escape might be possible. Now that she could see out of one eye, she found she could move better by rolling and shuffling across the floor. She reached the window and pulled awkwardly at the curtains with her teeth, until they opened enough for her see out.

She was in a ground floor room and there was a yard, some outbuildings and then woodland. She couldn't hear any traffic, so there obviously wasn't a main road nearby. It was getting dark, but she saw that Sarah's car was parked in the yard as was a small blue Renault with French number plates.

"What are you doing?" The loud, cross voice belonged to the woman, who had entered the room without Lottie noticing. Her raised voice brought the men to the room too, and Lottie had time to take in their appearances before they covered their faces. Both were probably in their thirties; one had dark hair combed back from his forehead, while the other was balding and wore glasses. The woman looked different. When she had picked Lottie up at school, she had worn large glasses and had dark hair. Now she had no glasses and her hair was short and fair. She must have been disguised when she first met Lottie.

"I'll put the blindfold back on her," said the woman.

"There is not a point now," responded the bald man. "She have seen us. She know our faces."

The dark-haired man turned to the other and said quietly, "Après le match, elle est morte."

"Silence! Pas devant l'enfant!" replied his comrade.

"Elle est anglaise. Elle ne parle pas francais!"

But as the adults left her in the room without her blindfold, but still bound at her wrists and ankles and now secured to the bed head with a rope, Lottie understood all too well what the men had said. Lottie had learned some French at school, but even more from her mother, who had been studying the language part-time at university and often practised her French with Lottie when they were alone together. She knew now that she had to get away as quickly as possible. Mort meant dead. After the match they were going to kill her, because she would be able to identify them if they didn't.

§

Her opportunity came sooner than she had expected. The woman came half an hour later with food: some bread and tomato soup. Lottie was too frightened to want to eat, but decided that she had to. She would need all of her strength and energy, if she was going to get away.

The woman told her she would untie her from the bed and take the tape from her wrists so that she could eat, but warned her that she had a gun and would not hesitate to use it if she had to. "Please don't make me, Lottie. I'd hate to have to shoot you."

Lottie resisted the temptation to ask what difference

it would make. The men were going to kill her anyway. She accepted the food. It was difficult to eat at first because her wrists ached from being bound, and she spilled some of the soup on the bed, but she gradually got used to moving her arms again and ate slowly while the woman sat in a chair watching her.

The men entered the room and spoke to the woman in French. She seemed to understand. "Nous allons en ville. Nous reviendrons dans moins d'une heure avec du vin et du pizza. OK?"

The woman nodded and took the gun from her pocket and showed it to them. "Pas de probleme. Quatre fromages pour moi, s'il vous plait."

Lottie listened but showed no sign of understanding, concentrating only on her soup as far as the kidnappers were concerned. But she knew that this was her best chance of escape. The men would be gone for up to an hour, which meant that all she had to do was escape from a woman with a gun. "Easy peasy," she thought sarcastically. "My ankles are bound, I don't know where I am, I'm held at gunpoint, and I have between about 30 minutes and an hour to get away!"

Lottie's mind raced. There had to be a way. The woman had been cross, but she didn't seem as bad as the men. Lottie wondered about pleading with her or promising she would never identify her if she'd just let her go, but decided that was very unlikely to work. No, escape was the only option, and first she had to get the woman to untie her legs. She waited until she heard the men drive away.

"I'm afraid I need the toilet," she said, putting on the politest voice she could muster.

"OK, I'll take you, but it's upstairs. You'll have to shuffle up the stairs on your bottom, because I'm not going to untie your legs. Either that or you can wait for the others to get back."

"But I need to go urgently."

"Oh God!" snapped the woman. She hesitated. "Right, your hands are free. You can take the tape off your ankles yourself. I'll keep hold of the gun. Don't make me use it, Lottie!"

Lottie picked at the black tape and then wound it back. It took about three minutes to remove it and her hands were sticky when her ankles were finally free. She still had no idea how she could escape without being shot. Her legs were even stiffer than her arms had been. Just trying to run away and dodge bullets wasn't an option. She'd need to find a way of giving herself a start, and she'd need time to get her legs working if she was to make a quick getaway. But perhaps the walk up the stairs might help, and then she would have to make her move.

Lottie struggled up the stairs, with the woman behind her waving the gun. "Second door on the left. Leave the door open," she said.

"No! I can't do that!" moaned Lottie in her most

plaintive voice. "I need to, you know... and I can't do that unless the door's closed."

"Stand aside!" barked the woman and backed into the room, her gun still trained on Lottie, who saw her look around the bathroom and check that the window was closed. "You have three minutes. You can close the door, but don't bolt it. And be sure to wash your hands!"

Despite being appalled at the suggestion that she might not wash her hands, Lottie decided to continue to be polite. "Thank you very much. I really appreciate this. I'll be as quick as I can."

Once inside the bathroom, Lottie surveyed it quickly. There was a bath, a sink and a toilet, and a metal bin. The window was closed but didn't seem to be locked, but she could see that it was a long drop to the ground. She'd almost certainly break her ankle or worse if she jumped. Then she noticed that there was a door next to the bath. Not a full-sized door, but one which was perhaps a metre and a half tall. As silently as possible, Lottie opened the door to discover that it was an airing cupboard with a hot water tank. The tank was lagged and there were sheets and blankets on a shelf above it. There was probably just enough room for her to climb inside and close the door. An idea formed very quickly.

"Haven't you finished yet? One more minute and I'm coming in," growled the woman from the other side of the bathroom door.

"Sorry, I won't be long." Lottie leaned against the bathroom door and silently slid the small bolt across. There was no sound from the woman, so she assumed she hadn't heard. The bolt was flimsy, but it might buy her a little time.

Then she looked around for the heaviest thing she could find and found the only thing available was the metal waste bin. Quickly, she pulled at the metal catch on the window. It resisted at first, but she managed to open it. Then, leaving it wide open, she hurled the bin from it to the ground below.

As she heard the woman outside swear and curse, Lottie clambered into the airing cupboard, pulled a blanket around her and drew the door closed.

"Lottie, what are you doing in there?" yelled the woman, but Lottie didn't answer. There was more cursing and then the woman tried to open the door. The bolt held and she threw herself against the door. It broke open. "Oh my God, the window!" she shrieked, and Lottie heard her footsteps rapidly descend the stairs.

She clambered out of the airing cupboard and peered around the door. The woman had gone. She must be heading outside to look for Lottie, who hoped she had assumed she had jumped from the window. She closed the bathroom door quietly.

As calmly as she could, Lottie crept down the stairs and found a living room below. On the table was a mobile phone. She picked it up and put it into her pocket. It might be useful later, but it might also prevent the woman from calling the men now. A door from the living room was open and through it Lottie could see a kitchen with a door which opened to the yard. The door was wide open. The woman must have gone through it to find out if Lottie had jumped from the bathroom window. Perhaps she was waiting outside now, or perhaps she was looking for her near the house. Either way, Lottie decided that it would be best to find another way out of the house. Her legs were now working fine and she moved swiftly to find the front door. It had a Yale lock, which she opened easily from the inside, and then stepped outside into the dusk.

She could make out a track, fields and trees. There were buildings around the house. Having surveyed the scene and looked around carefully for the woman, she chose a path leading to what appeared to be a very large wood, which lay around a hundred metres from the house. It was only when she was about twenty metres from the trees that she heard the woman shout, "Lottie, stop or I'll shoot!"

CHAPTER SIX

BECKY AND RACHEL

Just as we sometimes fall asleep for a only a very few minutes and yet have dreams which seem to last for hours, the thoughts which flashed through Lottie's mind as she sprinted those twenty metres into the woods seemed far too long and complicated to have in a few seconds. She thought of her mum.

The thoughts were random and disorganised, but at their heart was Lottie's love for and gratitude to her mother. Becky was almost still a child herself when Lottie was born, yet she had cared for her like someone much more mature. Becky was bright, intelligent, had a wonderful sense of humour and the most sparkly blue eyes Lottie had ever seen. She had a laugh which was infectious and often had the whole family, including grandparents and visitors, almost rolling on the floor with laughter with just one remark or one silly voice.

Becky could impersonate just about anyone, including Steve, and she often entertained the family with her impression of him after a match, exaggerating his Yorkshire accent and some of the phrases he used. "We just tek each game as it cooms. We never talk abart league tables" was one of the things he had said to an interviewer on Match of the Day, and for some reason Becky thought this was hilarious. And her impression of one of the French managers of a rival team had Steve's teammates crying with laughter when she did it at a club party. Rovers' manager asked her to do it every time he saw her, but she would only say one sentence like, "Oh no Meester MacGregor, eet is not posseeble for me to do zat." She also impersonated Mr MacGregor, but had the sense not to that when he was around!

Becky had given up a place at university to have Lottie, but now that they could afford to have Sarah look after Rachel so that she could go to lectures, she had begun a French course at the local university. She was very modest, but when she got the marks for her first essays, she almost burst with pride and they'd all gone out for pizza to celebrate. That night she didn't even mind the inevitable autograph hunters who seemed to come over to their table every two minutes.

Lottie's parents had planned to have Rachel, and often referred to her as "the miracle child", because she had been born eight weeks too soon, but had survived because of the care of the doctors and nurses and the wonderful incubator in the baby unit. No-one would ever have looked at four-year-old Rachel and thought that she had once been such a tiny baby who had almost died. She was now a bubbly, happy child with dark curls and bright brown eyes, who never seemed to be still. With seven years between them, Lottie saw Rachel as someone to look after and play with, and they rarely argued as they might have if they'd been closer in age.

Now, as she stumbled through the woods, pursued by a woman with a gun, Lottie wondered if she'd ever see her family again.

CHAPTER SEVEN
ON THE RUN

As she lay in the bracken watching the men and hoping they couldn't see her, Lottie was relieved to see them turn in the direction that the deer had run. Perhaps they thought that the noise and movement of the deer was the noise and movement of the girl they were trying to recapture, because they set off after them.

When Lottie had entered the woods, the woman seemed to have given up the chase and had probably gone back to the house to wait for the men and tell them what had happened. Lottie had tried to get as far from the house as possible as quickly as possible, but soon found she was lost and didn't know which direction to take. An hour after she had escaped, she found herself hiding in the bracken with the men nearby. She must still be near the house, she thought. An hour and she had got almost nowhere.

Suddenly, she heard the men again. They seemed to be coming back towards her. She crept through the bracken and looked into the darkness for a means of escape. The trees towered above her, their dark silhouettes draped with June leaves. A month later and Lottie knew that the leaf cover would have been heavier and the wood would have been even darker, and it would have been easier to hide but harder to find her way out. She searched for a tree to climb. Most seemed to have lost their lower branches and there was nothing climbable. Then, a little way off, she saw what she had been looking for. The tree, an oak, was at the edge of the clearing, but had low branches which she knew she could reach. She scrambled through the undergrowth and looked around frantically to see if the men were near.

When she was confident that she couldn't be seen, Lottie sprang up and grabbed the lowest branch. She'd always been good at climbing trees, but had never climbed one in the dark before. As she found a position on the lowest branch, she heard the men's voices again. They were getting nearer. Fear drove her on. She pulled herself up onto a higher branch and, making sure there was plenty of foliage to hide her, found herself a position from which she could see the clearing.

Seconds later, she saw them. They were walking slowly into the clearing, looking around them and listening. When they spoke, they did so quietly so that she knew they were speaking, but couldn't make out the words. When they reached the middle of the clearing, they stopped and stood close together. Lottie could tell they were planning something by the way they gestured and pointed. She saw one of them reach into his pocket and take out his mobile phone. He began to tap in numbers. Who could he be calling? thought Lottie, and realised as the phone in her pocket began to vibrate that it was her. They knew she'd taken the phone and were ringing its number to try to locate her position.

Lottie almost fell from the branch as she reached into her pocket, took out the phone and, bracing herself against the tree trunk, hurled it into the woods away from the clearing. It began ringing as it flew through the air.

The phone continued to ring after it had landed and the men looked around rapidly trying to trace where the sound was coming from. Lottie held her breath as they stumbled through the undergrowth below the tree and made their way towards the cheery tune of the ring tone. Its jolly sound was in sharp contrast to the state of terror in which Lottie found herself. The ringing stopped before the men found the phone. It must have gone to answerphone. As they stopped to dial the number again, Lottie wondered whether she should take the opportunity to jump from the tree and run away. Even before she had made up her mind, something happened which made the decision for her. There was a rustling and then the sound of running. The deer were back!

Again, the men followed them. Again, they mistook the sound of the deers' retreat for the sound of their prey. As they disappeared into the distance, Lottie seized her chance. She scrambled down from the tree, thought about looking for the mobile, but dismissed the idea because it would delay her, and ran through the clearing in the opposite direction from the one the men had taken.

CHAPTER EIGHT

CANCELLED

Ellie had been disappointed when she heard the answerphone message. Lottie's grandmother was very apologetic. She was really sorry, but Lottie wouldn't be able to stay that night because she had to go to visit her grandad, who was poorly.

Ellie had been looking forward to having Lottie to stay. They would have watched TV in her room and eaten pizza and drunk lemonade. They would have giggled and laughed until midnight or whenever Ellie's mum had come up to tell them to be quiet because they were keeping her awake. Ellie hoped Lottie's grandad would get well soon, but she couldn't help thinking that it was rather thoughtless of him to be ill that day.

CHAPTER NINE

OUT OF THE WOODS

The trouble was, she simply didn't know which way to go. The wood couldn't go on forever, but Lottie had no idea where she was or where she might find safety. The one thing she did know was that the further she was from the kidnappers, the safer she would be.

She cursed having her shorts on as she battled through nettles and brambles, and she knew her legs must be scratched and red if the soreness she felt was anything to go by. At least she was wearing trainers rather than school shoes, and this enabled her to move quite quickly whenever she freed herself from the tangled undergrowth. She was grateful that her games kit was in dark colours, which might make her harder to see, but the darkness made it hard to find a path. The wood didn't seem like one of those that the family had walked through where there were lots of footpaths and even signs to guide walkers. This wood was dense with occasional clearings where trees had been cut down and replaced by saplings. It didn't seem to have any footpaths at all.

Every few minutes she stopped and crouched down as quietly as she could, partly to catch her breath and partly to listen for sounds of her pursuers. There were only the sounds of the woods: occasional hoots from owls, shufflings and scratching of tiny animals, and the rustling of leaves in the light breeze. There was little moonlight to illuminate the way, so she carried on running, walking and stumbling in a direction which she thought was taking her away from the kidnappers.

After about thirty minutes, she thought she saw a light glowing and decided to head towards it. If there was a house, it might be at the edge of the woods. Perhaps there would be someone there to help her: someone who could contact the police and her parents.

The light grew larger and brighter as Lottie moved with even more determination towards it. Gradually, she made out the shape of a house and some outbuildings. She began to run, suddenly feeling that she was about to be safe and that the nightmare of the last few hours would soon be over. And then she froze. It was indeed a house and there were outbuildings. A light shone from a window and there were two cars outside: a Renault (probably blue, but she couldn't be sure in the darkness) and a Volvo, which she felt sure was Sarah's car, the one the kidnappers must have stolen to pick her up after school. She had gone round in a circle and had ended up back where she started. Lottie felt tears welling in her eyes as the frustration sank in, but she fought them back.

She told herself that she was still free. They hadn't found her yet and the last place they would probably think of looking was near the house she'd escaped from.

She crouched in the undergrowth and decided that she needed to think. It was no good simply running away. She needed a plan.

Her mother had often told her that when she had to make a big decision, she made two lists: one with the good things about each choice and one with the bad things. Lottie decided that she had two options: she could either go back into the woods and try to find another way out; or she could use the house as a starting point for finding a road and perhaps a town or village. She had no paper or pen, so she listed the advantages and disadvantages of each action in her head. If she went back into the woods, she might be safer but she wouldn't know where to go. She might wander about lost for hours and the kidnappers might find her when dawn arrived. She might even blunder into them and be recaptured.

If she started from near the house, she would probably find a track which led to a road. There had to be one for the cars to be there. She could circle the house at a distance until she found the track. On the other hand, she might be seen, especially if she actually walked or ran on the track. Lottie made her decision. Finding a track which led to a road was the only sure way to find a way out of the woods. There were disadvantages, but not as many as if she went back into the woods.

She crept through the trees, noticing that the

undergrowth wasn't as dense near to the house. When she was near to the lighted window she considered going up to it and trying to see if the crooks were in the house, but quickly dismissed the idea as too risky. Instead, she kept at least ten metres from the house and set off in a clockwise direction, always keeping an eye on the buildings as well as looking over her shoulders to check that she wasn't being watched.

A sudden noise, followed by the appearance of a long shaft of light, made her halt and dive for cover. Peering though the vegetation, she saw that a door had opened, and noticed the silhouette of the woman against the light. There was a red glow which brightened as Lottie watched. The woman had stepped out of the house to smoke a cigarette. Lottie watched for around five minutes and saw the woman lean against the door post with her head back as she blew smoke into the air. Her parents had told Lottie never to smoke and warned her about the dangers of all the illnesses which smokers suffered from. "At least if they all smoke," thought Lottie, "they might not be able to run fast enough to catch me!"

In fact, Lottie was pretty confident that she could outrun most people, including many adults. She had won every race she'd entered at the school sports and was the District Champion at 100 and 800 metres. The previous week she had won the 800 metres by such a distance at the District Sports that she had been having a drink from her water bottle and talking to her teacher when the person who came second crossed the finishing line. A grim determination flowed through her body. "If they want to catch me, they'll need to run faster than they've ever run before!" she thought.

At last, the woman went back indoors and closed the door. Lottie waited a moment and then continued to skirt the buildings until she found a gravelled track which she could see led to where the cars were parked. In the other direction it curved through some trees and then seemed to disappear down a hill. She kept her distance from the track but followed its route until she could see, perhaps half a mile away, the silhouettes of telegraph poles, trees and hedges. "There must be a road," she thought and began to make her way towards it. As the trees petered out, there was a short hedge with a field behind it. The sweet scent of flowers filled her nostrils as she crept along with the hedge between herself and the track. The plants were tall and grew almost right up to the hedge and she knew what they were: oil seed rape. Her mother often complained about the splashes of bright yellow in the countryside, which she described as "hideous". "They just don't look natural!" she moaned. "And besides, they make me sneeze!"

Lottie thought about her mother's words as she continued to descend towards the road. There was no sign of the kidnappers, but she knew that one sneeze could give her away, and just thinking about sneezing seemed to be making her feel that she needed to. She decided to try to move more quickly and had got to within a hundred metres of the road when she heard the sound of a car starting. Suddenly, the track was brightly lit by the full beam headlights of a car leaving the house. Lottie threw herself to the ground and crawled on her tummy deeper into the field and then lay still and panting among the tall stalks of the crop.

The car roared along the road and even in the darkness Lottie could tell that it threw up a cloud of dust behind it. The combination of the dust, the crop and her fear of sneezing were too much for her and she began to sneeze violently and repeatedly. She was sure she hadn't been heard above the noise of the car, but then she heard a squeal of brakes and saw a bright red glow coming from the track. The car had stopped. Had they heard her? There was silence, followed by a crunching mechanical noise and a white light from the car's reversing light as it moved backwards at speed.

CHAPTER TEN

DRIVING

Lottie heard the car come to a screeching halt, sending dust and pebbles in all directions. She heard the door open and the crunch of someone's feet on the gravel. The footsteps seemed to be moving away from her, but then they stopped. Lottie wanted to peer through the crop to see who was there, but she was frantically trying to stop herself from sneezing again. She was certain the driver must be one of the kidnappers. She needed to distract them if she was to get away.

Pinching her nose with one hand, she felt around on the ground until she put her hand on a rock the size of a cricket ball. Lottie was sure she was going to sneeze again and when it happened she wanted to divert the kidnapper's attention from her to somewhere else. She weighed the rock in her hand. At rounders and cricket she was known for having a good, strong throw. Now she needed to hurl the rock as far as possible, perhaps further than she'd ever thrown a rounders or cricket ball.

Carefully, gently, nervously, she rose from the

ground and peered towards the track. The car was the Renault and she could see the woman standing next to it scanning the fields on either side of her. She stood on the driver's side, the side opposite to where Lottie was hiding. Lottie watched and made lists in her head. It took only seconds for to decide what she would do. It was risky, but if it worked she would leave the crooks without one of their cars and get further from the house than she could ever hope to on foot.

Lottie knew how to drive. Her father had taught her in a small Toyota which he and she had driven around the grounds of their enormous house. She'd never driven very fast, but she knew how to steer, brake and change gear. Still fearful that she would sneeze, Lottie stood as tall as she could without letting her head rise above the crop. The woman was still near the car, but she had moved closer to the field opposite Lottie.

Lottie felt around for another rock. She'd need to throw one into the field and the second further into the field, so that the woman would think she was moving away from the road. It would need to be the longest throw she'd ever made. She weighed the rocks in her hands in turn. She put one back on the ground, stood carefully, made sure the woman wasn't looking in her direction, and then drew back her arm and hurled the rock with all her might. She watched, trying to spot the rock in the darkness, but lost track of it before it thudded to the ground in the field opposite. The woman was startled. She peered into the field and then seemed to make up her mind. As the woman set off into the crop, Lottie crept, rock in hand, as quickly and quietly as she could towards the car. When she was at the edge of the track, Lottie hurled the second rock, once again putting all of her strength into her throw. The woman stopped and then moved further into the field.

Lottie knew she had to be quick. Once the woman heard the car start, she'd get back to it rapidly. When she opened the door, the interior light would come on. She had to open the door quickly and climb in and close it and hope the woman didn't see the light from the field. Lottie took a deep breath, leapt from the field to the car, opened the driver's door and climbed in. She froze in horror. There was no steering wheel, no dials in front of her and no ignition key! Then she realised. How could she have been so stupid? She'd seen the car had French number plates. She should have known the steering wheel would have been on the left-hand side!

It was too late to get out of the car and go round to the other side, so she clambered over into the other front seat, banging her knee sharply on the gear stick as she did so. She looked out of the window. There was no sign of the woman. She felt for the ignition key.

It wasn't in the same place as on the Toyota. In fact, nothing seemed to be in the same place. The gear stick was on her right instead of her left. She wondered if the accelerator, brake and clutch would be in the same order and felt for them with her feet. Even though she was tall for her age, the woman was taller and Lottie realised that the seat was too far back for her to reach the pedals properly.

Frantically, she felt under the seat for the lever which adjusted the seat. She couldn't find it. Nothing was going according to plan, and then things got worse. About twenty metres ahead of her, at the side of the road, the woman emerged from the field. Lottie had to act immediately or be captured.

Lottie grabbed the seat belt and fastened it, then sat at the edge of the seat and stretched her legs to reach what she hoped were the clutch and accelerator. She pushed the clutch in as far as she could make it go, and forced the car into gear, praying that she had chosen first gear and not fifth. She wanted to be all ready to go as soon as she started the engine, and she wanted to do that last because she knew the noise would be heard by the woman. Finally, she turned the ignition key and the car burst into life. She saw the woman turn and begin running towards the car.

Lottie let out the clutch and the car jerked forward and almost stalled before she thrust down her right foot onto the accelerator. She had chosen correctly. The pedals were in the same order as on a right-hand drive car and she seemed to be in first gear, because the car began to move a little less jerkily.

Again, Lottie pushed in the clutch and then pulled the gear stick back into second before pressing harder on the accelerator. It was so dark that she could hardly see the road in front of her, but she could see enough to glimpse the woman diving out of the way as the little Renault growled towards her.

Now Lottie fumbled for the headlights as she manoeuvred the car along the dark track. It was difficult enough driving in the dark, sitting on the wrong side of the car and worrying about the woman chasing her, without having to find instruments, but finally she managed to turn on the lights and saw that she was rapidly approaching the end of the track and the road. She knew she shouldn't drive on the road. She should abandon the car and run, and be grateful that it had put some distance between herself and the woman. She could be killed or might kill someone else. Driving around the grounds of her house was one thing, but she had no idea about how to drive when there was other traffic around. A few metres from the end of the track she brought the car to a stop and, after a struggle, put the handbrake on and turned off the ignition. She climbed from the car and was about to start running when she heard footsteps and looked around to see the shadowy figure of the woman running down the track, perhaps a hundred metres away.

CHAPTER ELEVEN

LUCKY LOTTIE

As she stood as still as she could in the shadows, Lottie was aware of the rhythm of her beating heart. It seemed so loud, she felt sure the people looking for her must hear it from miles away.

"Lot-tie, Lot-tie, Lot-tie, here is Lot-tie," it seemed to thump out. Then after a while she found she was fitting the words of the nickname her friends sometimes used: "Luck-y Lot-tie, Luck-y Lot-tie." She started to think about the first time they'd called her that, after sports day in Year 5: Bella and Ellie banging her on the back and getting all the others to chant as she went up to be awarded the Y5 Cup.

But it wasn't just the sport. Lottie had always known that she was different from the other children she knew. It wasn't just that she could run faster, throw further and seemed to learn more quickly than almost everyone else in her class. It wasn't simply that she had a famous father, a clever mother, a big house and went on holiday to exotic places where the family stayed in the best hotels and ate wonderful food. Lottie knew that people noticed her for another reason: the colour of her skin.

It wasn't that people mentioned it all the time or even very often. At school, there had only been a handful of occasions when anyone had even mentioned Lottie's brown skin, and even then no-one had ever been deliberately unkind or cruel about it. She didn't expect them to be. Some people had freckles, some had ginger hair, some wore glasses, a boy in year 4 was in a wheelchair. Everyone was different. Everyone was unique. If no-one teased, bullied or taunted brown-haired kids, why would they be cruel to someone with brown skin? That's what her mother had said and, on the whole, that's what Lottie had found. But still, Lottie always felt that she was different.

She could remember little incidents which had etched themselves in her memory and which reminded her that she was different. There had been the little boy in Year 1 who had rubbed her hand to see if he could make the brown colour come off. "Are you dirty?" he had asked. Lottie had laughed at the time, but even though she knew the boy hadn't meant to be unkind, she had been hurt by what he had said. She was the only child in the school with brown skin. It was only natural that a five-year-old who only ever saw white-skinned children would be curious. But still she felt unhappy that her skin colour had been noticed and commented upon.

Worse by far was the woman who had talked to her and her mother in the restaurant after a Rovers match. Perhaps she had thought she was being pleasant, but Lottie didn't think so. Talking about Lottie as if she wasn't there, the woman had said to her mother, "She seems quite bright for a… you know…" she had hesitated and Lottie's mother had interrupted sharply.

"No, I don't know Mrs Forsythe. Tell me!"

Mrs Forsythe had blushed and stumbled over her words. "For a, well, you know, coloured child."

"Mrs Forsythe," said Lottie's mother in the calm but angry voice Lottie only heard when she had been particularly naughty, "my child is very bright full stop. She happens to have brown skin and that's because my husband has black skin and I have white skin. At the moment, you have very red skin because you are blushing so much because you know, or at least I hope you know, that you have just said something really stupid."

Mrs Forsythe was almost shaking with anger as she began, "Well, I… you're all the same you people…", but Lottie's mother had taken her daughter by the hand and was walking briskly out of the restaurant before Lottie could hear any more.

There had been other minor incidents which Lottie had stored away in her memory and which had troubled her a lot at the time, but far less after she had talked about them with her parents. On school trips, some shopkeepers seemed to pay her a little more attention than her friends, perhaps thinking that she might be a shoplifter. After she had won the 100 metres race at the District Sports, she was sure she had heard one of the other girls' fathers say, "Of course she won, she's black. But you came first out of the white kids."

When she'd asked her parents what the man had meant, they had told her the man was an idiot, but that it was true that brown and black athletes did win most of the races at the Olympics.

"Did people say things to you about the colour of your skin when you were a kid, Dad?" Lottie had asked. And her father had told her that he'd spent most of his childhood in fights because people had called him names or told him to go back to Jamaica.

"I wouldn't mind," he'd said, "but I was born and brought up in Yorkshire and so was my dad. I've got a Yorkshire accent and I'd never even been to Jamaica until I played there for England. It's a great place though. We'll go there for a holiday one day."

"But people shouldn't say things to you because of the colour of your skin, should they Dad."

"No love, they shouldn't. But they say things about the colour of their hair, the length of their noses, their height, their spectacles and even their clothes, so maybe it's not quite as bad as you might think. You know Wayne Moxon, our best striker, he's going bald and the lads tease him about it every day at training. It doesn't mean they don't like him. People just like to comment on things that are different."

"Do people still say things about you being black, Dad?"

"Sometimes, but usually they don't mean to be unkind. Like when I was made captain of England and Jermaine Tilson was made vice captain, they had headlines in the papers like "Blacktastic" and "Black Power!" We thought it was great, but some people were really offended and wrote letters to the newspapers complaining."

Her father was more talkative than usual and he went on, "But when they printed a picture of Mark Watson moaning at the referee, they had the headline "Ginger Whinger" because of his hair, and you know how Mr Macgregor has a long nose?"

"Yes."

"Well he got really upset when the paper printed a picture of him rubbing it, with the caption, "He Nose a Thing or Two". One of the lads cut it out and pinned it on the noticeboard, but it disappeared very quickly!"

"Just the same, Lottie," interrupted her mother, "whatever anyone says to you or calls you, you should never go down to their level by calling them things back."

And Lottie had stored away that particular conversation with her parents, and had secretly vowed that she would never deliberately say anything just to hurt someone because they looked different from other people. She knew that she was not only different, she was lucky. She was fit, healthy, clever, and her parents were wealthy. She'd never starve like millions of people, and she had a family who loved her and cared for her, which many children didn't have. Lottie decided that she was who she was, and she was proud of it. Lucky Lottie, that's who she was!

"I'm Lucky Lottie," she told herself, "and I'm going to get out of this. I'm Lucky Lottie and I'm going home!"

CHAPTER TWELVE

RUN OR DRIVE

Lottie felt anything but lucky as she watched the woman start to run towards her. She had to make up her mind quickly. Run or drive. Those were her only options and there was hardly time to think too much about advantages and disadvantages.

She chose to drive.

The car burst into life again as she started it, but she was in too much of a hurry and stalled the engine as soon as she tried to make it move forward. "Calm down, Lottie!" she said aloud, and started the car again. This time she managed to make it move and she could see the figure of the woman getting smaller when she looked in the mirror.

All too soon, Lottie reached the road. She stopped the car and looked carefully to the left and right. She'd cycled on roads with her mother so she had some idea about the Highway Code, but this was different.

There was nothing else on the road, so she turned to the left and began to drive slowly, keeping well to the left. She thought it would seem very strange for someone who was used to driving in Britain to be sitting on the left-hand side of a car, but she had never sat anywhere else when she had been in the front of her parents' cars, so it almost seemed the natural place to be. The thing that didn't seem natural was having the steering wheel in front of her and being in control of the car.

The car began to make a lot of noise as Lottie grew in confidence and pressed harder on the accelerator. She knew she had to change gear. Getting from first to second had been easy, but putting the car into third gear was much harder. She'd always struggled with that when driving the Toyota. You had to move the gear stick forward, then to the right and then forward again, all the time pressing on the clutch, before letting the clutch out smoothly. Her father was very patient, but even he had begun to get slightly irritated one day when Lottie kept making the car do what he called kangaroo jumps as she tried repeatedly to change into third gear.

There was still no other traffic around, so she decided she would change gear. Her father had always told her not to look at the gear stick when changing gear, but that was much easier when she was used to it being on her left. Now she had to feel around for it, and when she looked down the car swerved and bumped as the wheels went onto the grass verge. Lottie was shaken and her hand trembled as she fumbled for the gear lever again. This time she found it and managed to keep steering in a straight line as she depressed the clutch and pushed the lever forward, but when she tried to move it across and into third gear, she struggled. There were grating noises and the car slowed down. She tried again, but just couldn't do it and the car had almost stopped by the time she forced the lever forward.

It jerked and roared and Lottie knew that she had put it into first gear not third. This was too difficult. She knew she had to abandon the car and continue her escape on foot.

The car crept along in first gear as Lottie looked around for somewhere to stop. At last, she found a gateway to a field and pulled over onto the grass verge. Still shaking with fear after the drive, Lottie climbed out of the car and closed the door. Then she opened it again, took out the ignition key and locked the door. The car was old and she wasn't sure if it had central locking, so she waked around to the other side and locked that door too. There were no rear doors. Finally, she looked around her and saw that the road didn't have white lines in the middle and was clearly not a main road.

She stood still looking at the hedges at the side of the road and the dark, undulating, hilly fields behind them. There was no sign of a house and the only sound was the wind rustling though the hedgerows. She was alone, afraid and frightened. Somewhere, probably not very far away, were three people who were dangerous and who would probably kill her if they found her, to prevent her from identifying them. Lottie needed another plan, and she needed one quickly.

CHAPTER THIRTEEN
RATS

The first thing she needed to do was to get as far away from the car as possible as quickly as possible. If the men came along the road in the other car, they'd be bound to stop when they saw the Renault.

Lottie weighed the keys in her hand and, for the fourth time that night, made use of her throwing skills. The keys flew over the nearest hedge and deep into a field. She was sure the kidnappers would never find them, at least not in the dark, and that meant they now had only one car as well as being short of one mobile phone.

Lottie listened intently for the sound of distant cars and, when she heard nothing, began to walk quickly and then, when her legs began to feel better, run along the road. She stopped regularly, both to listen for cars and to get her breath back.

Above her, The moon was a small fingernail peeping out behind clouds and distant stars twinkled. She saw the flashing red light of an aeroplane moving across the dark sky, occasionally disappearing as it passed behind a cloud. Up there were people laughing, talking, perhaps on their way to a warm sunny holiday. They were only a few miles from where Lottie trudged along the road, her head flicking back and forth as she examined every shadow for signs of danger. They were so near, but might as well have been a million miles away for all the help they could give her.

After about twenty minutes, she came to a crossroads. There was a sign with the names of towns or villages, but it was difficult to read in the darkness. She was about to give up, and had just decided to take the right-hand turn, when she heard the sound of a vehicle in the distance. There were hedges at the sides of each of the roads and she looked for a gap to go through. There wasn't one. She'd be seen by whoever was driving! If the vehicle contained the kidnappers, that would be the end of her few hours of freedom and probably of her life.

Frantically, Lottie looked around for a hiding place. The lights of the vehicle were beginning to illuminate the road ahead. At the side of the road to the right she could just about make out a drainage ditch. She knew it was probably full of water, but it was her only chance. She could just see the headlights when she made her decision. As she scrambled down the bank of the ditch she felt dampness and then wetness seeping and soaking its way into her socks and trainers. The ditch was muddy and smelly and she heard rustling noises when she crouched as still as she could in the water.

Lottie stifled a scream as the rapidly approaching headlights lit the ditch and revealed the figures of two large water rats only a metre from where she lay. They seemed as startled as she was and quickly, and almost silently, retreated into the long grass at the water's edge.

Then the lights were gone and the roar of the vehicle gradually diminished as it sped into the distance. Perhaps she should have tried to wave the vehicle down. Perhaps the driver would have helped her. Perhaps he or she would have taken her to the nearest police station and she would have been given food and a hot drink while she waited for her mother to pick her up. And perhaps the car was driven by the kidnappers or by someone else who might have harmed her. Lottie knew she had made the right decision, and as she slipped and slid her way out of the ditch, her trainers full of water, her socks and shorts soaked and muddy, she knew that she needed to find a town or village when daylight came and she could go to a police station or a shop and ask for help. But where was the nearest town or village? She couldn't read the sign and had no idea where she was. In fact, even if she could read the sign, she might not have heard of the places shown on it. As she trudged and squelched her way along the road, heading for she didn't know where, Lottie wondered how long she had been unconscious after she had been kidnapped. How far could they have driven her? In an hour they might have travelled sixty miles, even more if they'd used a motorway. She could be more than a hundred miles from home. Even if she was nearer, she wasn't sure she would have heard of anywhere but the largest towns. Lottie fought against the feeling of hopelessness and helplessness which was beginning to engulf her.

She thought of her family. Her father wouldn't have given up. Look how hard he'd worked to become a top class footballer. Her mother wouldn't have given up. She'd been a mother at seventeen and had cared for Lottie when some people had suggested she should have had her adopted by another family. Even her sister, Rachel, was a fighter. She had fought for her own life as a tiny premature baby and she had survived. Lottie suddenly felt a new determination from somewhere deep inside her. She was going to survive.

CHAPTER FOURTEEN

ELLIE

Lottie decided she would turn her mind to happy thoughts to help her keep her spirits high. And there was no-one outside her family who made her happier than her friend, Ellie Snowden.

Ellie was a twinkly, smily person who could make anyone laugh, including teachers. Nothing ever seemed to upset her and everyone wanted to be her friend. But Lottie was her *best* friend. Lottie had lots of friends, but she knew that some people sought her friendship because she had a famous father. She was always being invited to parties and to other children's houses, but she could tell sometimes that people were disappointed if it was her mother who picked her up afterwards. She knew that they wanted to tell their friends that the England football captain, Steve Parry, had been to their house. And when her father did collect her, some people became rather nervous and talked too much, and she felt embarrassed for them.

Ellie wasn't like that at all. She wasn't interested in football and she certainly wasn't in awe of Steve. He loved the funny things she said and the jokes she told.

Ellie was the best joke-teller Lottie knew, and Steve used to say, "That girl will be on the telly one day. She's a natural comedian!"

Lottie tried to think of some of Ellie's jokes as she walked along the gloomy road. The one about the talking budgerigar was her favourite. Ellie told it brilliantly, doing different voices for the pet shop owner and the customer. Lottie tried to hear Ellie telling the joke, as she tramped along the road.

A man went to a pet shop and he bought a talking budgie. A week late he went back and said to the pet shop owner, "That talking budgie you sold me, it hasn't said a word." (Ellie said did this with a very broad northern accent).

The pet shop owner said (in a rather posh voice), "Tell me sir, does he tap his beak on his little mirror?"

"He hasn't got a mirror!"

"Ah well, Sir, perhaps you'd better buy one if you want him to talk."

So the man buys a mirror and takes it home, but a week later he's back.

"That talking budgie you sold me," he moaned, "it still hasn't said a word!"

"Tell me Sir, does he swing on his little swing?" asked the pet shop owner.

"He hasn't got a swing!"

"Ah well, Sir, no wonder he isn't talking. Shall I sell you a swing?"

And the man bought a swing and took it home.

A week later he returned. "That talking budgie's still not talking," he grumbled.

"Tell me Sir, does he ring his little bell?

"Bell?" said the man. "He hasn't got a bell!"

So the man bought a bell and took it home.

A week later he came back to the pet shop looking very downcast.

"Whatever is the matter, Sir?" asked the pet shop owner.

"It's that talking budgie you sold me: it died!"

"Oh dear, Sir, I am sorry. Tell me, did it say anything before it died?"

"Yes," said the man.

"And what did it say, Sir?"

The man looked embarrassed. "It said, 'Don't they sell any blinking bird seed at that pet shop?'"

When Lottie had tried to tell Ellie's joke to other people they had hardly laughed. When Ellie told it they almost fell about laughing.

If only Ellie were with her now, telling jokes and making her laugh; taking her mind off the fear and the darkness; and the rustlings and scufflings in the hedgerows and the constant feeling that someone or something would emerge from the shadows and hurt her. Together, they would have made a game of walking down an unlit lane. Ellie would have made up jokes about ghosts and bogey men and wild animals, and they would have shrieked and giggled and walked hand in hand.

There could be no giggling now. Lottie was even conscious of trying to tread softly on the road so as not to attract attention. She didn't know where she was and she didn't know where she was going. All she knew was that she must keep moving and keep out of sight until daylight.

The road narrowed and the hedgerows grew taller and seemed to be closing in around her, almost like a tunnel. Suddenly, she stopped. There was movement behind the hedge to her right: movement and noise. She stood absolutely rigid with fear, certain once again that her heartbeat would be heard by whoever was behind the hedge.

There was a snuffling sound accompanied by a movement in the shadows close to the ground. Lottie backed slowly away from the sound, thinking that she might hide in the dark shadows of the opposite hedge. But she froze when the noise grew louder. Then she saw it. A badger! She'd never seen one outside the pages of a book. It was bigger than she had expected and it trundled out of the hedge and the long grass and began to cross the road. Lottie was transfixed. It was the size of a small dog, but it moved in a rather lumbering and awkward way. She was only a couple of metres away from it, but it didn't seem to have noticed her. There were more fumblings and crunchings as two more, smaller badgers emerged from the undergrowth and followed the larger one across the road and into the hedge opposite. Then they were gone and the sounds of their movement receded. Lottie was alone again, relieved that it had not been her captors who had disturbed the silence; elated that she had seen another wild animal at close quarters. First the deer, then the water rats, now the badgers: she couldn't wait to tell her mum and Rachel. But then she realised that she might never see them again, and an overwhelming sense of sadness fell upon her.

Once again, she began to walk along the road, but now tiredness began to take hold of her. It must be long past her usual bedtime. The only sleep she had had since seven that morning had been induced by some sort of drug the kidnappers had given her when she was captured. Now, she knew that she would not be able to keep walking for much longer. She needed to find shelter and a place to rest, but it had to be somewhere where she would not be found: perhaps a barn or some other farm building, or maybe a deserted house.

The hedges were still too thick and high for her to be able to see through them and find a shelter. Tiredness overtook her rapidly. Her legs ached and felt heavy. She found she couldn't stop herself from yawning over and over again, although she tried desperately hard not to make a noise when she did. She felt her eyes beginning to close so that she was almost walking in her sleep.

Her head began to swim and she felt increasingly dizzy. Lottie knew she couldn't walk much further.

Then she saw a gap in the hedge. There was a track. It must be a farm track, because she could tell that it had grass in the middle and there were puddles in the ruts at either side. There was no sign and nothing to indicate where the track might lead, but she decided to take it. It might lead to a farm and there might be somewhere there for her to hide while she regained her energy. Most of all, it was off the road and she was less likely to be spotted by kidnappers in a car.

In the darkness, she found it difficult to avoid the puddles and repeatedly splashed into them. Some were deep and the water came over her ankles. Then she'd be back on the dry earthy surface again, her socks and trainers soaked. Her feet had only just begun to feel dry after her earlier encounter with the ditch. Now the discomfort added to her tiredness made her feel gloomy and dejected. She wanted to sit at the side of the track and cry, but she forced herself to go on.

The track emerged from hedgerows into an area of almost flat, open land. There were crops in the fields, but in the darkness she couldn't tell what they were: corn or barley perhaps? Lottie looked at them to see if they might offer a hiding place if she thought her kidnappers were close. The crops were only about half a metre tall: she would have to lie flat if she wasn't to be seen. And even if she stayed in that position, she wouldn't be able to move when dawn broke because there was nothing to hide behind.

Just as Lottie was on the verge of tears, her spirits lifted. There was a building about fifty metres away to her left. She could make out its silhouette. There was no light and it seemed too small to be a house. She made up her mind. She had to rest and shelter. She looked for a path or a track which would lead to the building, but when she found nothing, decided to walk through the crops. Her legs were scratched and chafed by the grassy plants and she knew she was making a lot of noise as she staggered and stumbled towards the building, but she had started so she would finish.

She stopped regularly to scan the building and check for signs of life. There were none. As she neared it, she realised that it was deserted. It was made of brick and had a pointed, sloping roof, but although it had windows, there was no glass in them. The crop grew right up to an opening in the wall, which had no door. Lottie crept towards it, her tiredness and fatigue replaced by anxiety as she prepared to find out what lay inside.

CHAPTER FIFTEEN
SPIDERS

Lottie had never liked spiders. It wasn't that she thought they might hurt her. The ones in England weren't dangerous like some of those in Australia or Africa. It was something to do with the way they moved. All those long legs working together as they crawled across the floor or along a web: they never failed to make her stomach churn.

Her mum was the same, and her dad was often summoned to remove spiders from the bath before either of them would use the bathroom. But he wasn't allowed to kill them. Lottie and Becky didn't like spiders, but they didn't want to hurt them, so Steve had to catch them carefully in his cupped hands and then take them outside and set them free. "It's more than they'd do for the flies they catch!" laughed Steve more than once. But Lottie and Becky were adamant: one of Becky's favourite poems was *Hurt No Living Thing* by Christina Rossetti, and she often read it to the girls:

Hurt no living thing;
Ladybird, nor butterfly,
Nor moth with dusty wing,
Nor cricket chirping cheerily,
Nor grasshopper so light of leap,
Nor dancing gnat, nor beetle fat,
Nor harmless worms that creep.

So Lottie grew up being afraid of spiders, but would never dream of harming them.

Now her nerve was really being tested. As she cautiously peered into the building, she felt something touch her face. She started, then brushed whatever it was aside, but when she moved forwards she realised, even in the gloom, that there were cobwebs all around her. And where there were cobwebs, there must be spiders.

Lottie had just about made up her mind to leave the building and retrace her steps to the track, when the sound reached her ears. A car! Somewhere, not too far away, there was a car or a vehicle of some kind. She shrank into the building, putting aside her hatred of the cobwebs, as she was seized by the fear of something worse.

Suddenly, there was light. Light which seemed to bounce from land to sky as it illuminated the ground and then the sky. There was a vehicle moving along the track, the uneven surface making its headlights appear

to be moving up and down. Then the lights were still. The vehicle had stopped. As she peered around the wall, Lottie saw the interior light come on as the doors opened and two people got out, followed closely by two dogs. They were both men. The headlights were switched off and the men became less distinct in the darkness until two lights came on: they were carrying torches and Lottie could see that each was carrying something else too. Even from fifty metres away, she knew what they were. Rifles. They were armed and they had dogs. Dogs could follow a scent. Her scent. Lottie trembled with fear as she contemplated her last few moments of freedom and what might happen next.

CHAPTER SIXTEEN
HUNTED

Lottie listened intently. She wanted to hear what the men said. She wanted to know if they were her kidnappers. But the only thing she heard was shouts which sounded like "E-C, E-C". This was followed by the dogs running back from the fields to their masters.

It seemed a strange thing to call to dogs. Perhaps, thought Lottie, one was called E and one was called C. Even in her terrified state, she managed to feel some sympathy for the dogs. Ellie would have made a joke about it: probably something to do with a dog called B getting mixed up with an insect, she thought.

Then, to Lottie's amazement and huge relief, the men set off along the track away from the building where she hid. She heard the crunch and occasional splash of their boots growing softer as they got further away, and she watched the torch light suddenly veer away from the track and heard the dogs bark. Two cracks of gunfire split the air, followed by the sound of the dogs running. Then the men, dogs and the torchlight disappeared from view as if they had crossed the brow of a hill. She was safe for a little while longer.

Lottie made up her mind quickly. She was tired and her feet were wet, but she was also suddenly aware of being hungry: very hungry. Perhaps there would be something to eat in the car. The men and dogs were far enough away for her to reach the car and have a look. But had they locked it? She didn't recall seeing the indicator lights flash, as they did on many cars when they were locked using a remote control. She stepped out of the building, looked around carefully, and then ran as fast as she could through the crop to the car.

As she neared it, she saw that it was a four-wheel drive: a large off-the-road vehicle with big wheels and tyres. Any thought she might have had of trying her hand at driving again vanished at the sight of the car. The Renault had been difficult enough; this would be impossible.

She kept to the side of the car furthest away from where the men had gone with the dogs, and crept up to the front door on the passenger side. After peering into the darkness and reassuring herself that they were not in sight, she reached for the door handle. At first it wouldn't open, but then she found a lever behind the handle and squeezed it. There was a click and, as she pulled the handle, the door opened. The interior light came on and she was amazed to see that, once again, the steering wheel was on the left-hand-side. She climbed onto a step beneath the door and clambered into the vehicle, quickly glancing around for signs of food or anything which might be useful. There was a bar of chocolate in a tray between the seats and, just as she reached for it, she shrieked. But no-one heard her shriek. That would have been impossible above the noise of the car alarm. It wailed and screamed and screeched, making her ears vibrate and filling her head with noise.

Lottie grabbed the chocolate and ran. She ran through the field and past the building, trying to put as much distance as possible between her and the men with dogs and guns. They would certainly have heard the alarm and would surely be rushing back to find out what had set it off.

Lottie forgot her tiredness and ignored the scratches the crop made on her legs, as she hurtled through the grass. She ran and ran until she felt a stitch in her tummy and doubled up with her hands on her knees, gasping for breath. As she recovered, she looked back across the field to see if she was being followed. But there was no sign of the men, the dogs or the car: just a huge field which rose gently away from her to the silhouette of a hill against the night sky. Was she safe again? What about the dogs? Were the men looking for her or were they, perhaps, hunting for something else? But if they weren't looking for her before, maybe they would be now. She wondered if she had closed the door when she left the car. If she had, they might think the alarm had gone off by accident. That was always happening. Her mother had had a car with an alarm so temperamental that she finally changed it, because she was sick of having to go out to car parks and to the drive to try to stop it.

But she had taken the chocolate. Would they notice? Lottie felt the bar in her hand. The wrapper had been opened and some of the chocolate had been eaten, but there seemed to be plenty left. She remembered her hunger and tore at the wrapper and broke off a piece of chocolate. Even in the cool night air, the chocolate was rather melty in places from being held tightly in her hand as she had made her getaway. But that didn't prevent her from eating it. Never had she tasted chocolate like it. It was bitter and sweet at the same time and it melted further in her mouth as her hunger made her eat it greedily. One piece wasn't enough. She needed more, but first she needed shelter and a place to rest.

She looked around her. Back the way she had come were fields: huge fields with no hedges, but ahead of her she could make out trees and what looked like the silhouette of a building. It was, perhaps, a quarter of a mile away, but she summoned up what energy she had left – the chocolate seemed to have given her more – and began to tramp towards it.

As she neared the building, Lottie saw that there were others beyond it. Could there be a village? A police station? She moved cautiously. Besides finding safety and help, she was all too aware that she might also be found by the kidnappers.

When she reached a hedge and trees on the other side of which were buildings, Lottie pressed her back against a tree and peered through the hedge. She could see a farmyard and could just make out a tractor and a large combine harvester. There was a huge barn with what looked like a chimney on top and two large cylindrical silos stood to the left. She strained to listen for sounds of people or animals but there was only silence punctuated by the occasional very distant sound of a car on a far away road. She decided to head for the barn. If there was no-one around, she could shelter there. Perhaps there would be bales of hay to lie on. Maybe she could hide and get some sleep and then find a helpful farmer when day broke.

Lottie crept carefully along the hedge looking for a gap she could climb through. The trees and bushes were close to each other and there were nettles which stung her legs and almost made her cry out loud, but she carried on. It would be worth suffering a few stings and scratches to find somewhere to lie down.

Finally, she found a gap in the hedge, but had to fight back tears of frustration when she saw that there was a barbed wire fence filling it. It wasn't very high, and only came up to her chest, but when she tried to climb it it rocked and creaked so much that she quickly jumped down and hurried away further along the hedge.

She was now at the back of the barn, with the tractor and combine out of view. She hadn't yet seen a house. Perhaps no-one lived there and it was just a place where the farmer worked and stored his machinery. If it was, she would be able to rest undisturbed.

Suddenly, from somewhere not far away, the silence of the night was broken by an owl hooting, and then by rustling in the undergrowth. Lottie instinctively looked up. Yet again she saw wildlife which made her stop in her tracks. Against the dark night sky a large white barn owl glided swiftly and serenely before plunging to the ground. Lottie knew that some unfortunate small creature's life was probably ending as the hunter found its prey. In her present predicament, she felt a lot of sympathy for the creature. Like her, it was smaller than its predators and probably spent most of its time looking out for them as it tried to survive. The owl had been beautiful and it had to eat to survive. But Lottie knew that the people who were trying to catch her were just greedy. They wanted her because they could make money by getting her father to do something he would never have done, unless his daughter was in danger.

She wondered what her father would be doing now. He was staying in a hotel somewhere north of London with his England team mates. They always went to bed early the night before a match, but she knew Steve would be finding it hard to sleep. The players shared rooms. Would Steve tell his team mate about the kidnap? Would he tell him what he'd been told he must do if his daughter's life was to be saved? He couldn't know, as Lottie did, that the kidnappers meant to kill her anyway. She wanted to call him and tell him she was safe, or at least that she had escaped. She still didn't feel safe. She wanted to tell him not to let Andorra score twice. But she had no phone and had little chance of finding one before morning.

And then she found a tall, metal gate. It was fastened and she knew that opening it might be noisy and disturb someone, so she climbed it as quietly as she could. When she perched on the top she looked around the farmyard and took in the shadowy darkness of the barns and outbuildings; the abandoned farm machinery; and a large pile of what looked like tyres on top of a mound. She listened, but heard nothing apart from the distant hoot of an owl. Perhaps it was celebrating finding a tasty meal, thought Lottie, wishing that she had eaten more than a square of chocolate and a few mouthfuls of soup in the last few hours.

She lowered herself gently and quietly to the ground inside the farmyard and listened again. Nothing. She decided to head for the largest of the buildings, the barn, and began to move across the stony yard. And then the silence was shattered. An explosion of barking and growling, closely followed by the sight of two large dogs hurtling towards her from the direction of the barn, made her cry out loud in terror. Without having time to think, Lottie turned and sprinted back to the gate, grabbing at the top bar and hauling herself up just as the dogs reached her. She felt the wet nose of one them on the back of her leg as she flung herself over the bar and onto the other side. There was a sharp pain in her ankle as she landed, but her fear of the dogs forced her to drag herself to her feet. As she did so, she turned to see two large Alsatians leaping repeatedly at the gate, desperate to get over it to attack her.

The barking would surely wake someone, if indeed anyone lived at the farm, and Lottie didn't want to risk having the dogs set upon her. She was also unsure if the gate was high enough to keep the animals from her, so she hobbled, limped and then ran and limped as fast as she could to put as much distance as possible between herself and the farm as possible. And then, when she was perhaps two hundred metres from the gate, at the edge of the field, she saw something which lifted her spirits. Beyond the hedge she could make out more buildings; houses, and the tower and spire of a church. She had found a village at last. If she could just find somewhere to hide until daylight, she would be able to find help. She was going to survive. She was going to be safe.

She was going to get a message to her father before the match and before he did something dreadful.

Forgetting the pain in her ankle, Lottie marched along the hedge looking for another gap. The barking had subsided and she felt sure the dogs hadn't followed her. It was still very dark, but Lottie began to think that there was light at the end of the tunnel of problems which she had been through that night.

CHAPTER SEVENTEEN
THE FORD

Things went from good to better when, within seconds of spotting the village, Lottie found a gate which she could climb to reach a narrow tree-lined road. She used her left foot to step onto the gate, as her right ankle was still sore, and she clambered awkwardly over, taking care to ease herself gently, left foot first, to the ground. The village was to her left, and after a quick look up and down the road, she began to walk towards it. And then, when she was perhaps only a hundred metres away from the first house, she heard the car. It was coming towards her from the village.

The driver might be someone who could help her, but he or she might also be a kidnapper. She couldn't risk being seen. She needed daylight so that she could see who was who. Once again, Lottie found herself looking around desperately to find a hiding place. Then, twenty metres away, she saw that the road crossed a stream. There was a narrow humped back bridge, only wide enough for the smallest of vehicles, on the right, and to the left the road actually seemed to go through the stream. The lights of the car began to illuminate the hedges even before it came into view. Lottie made her decision. She ran as fast as her injured ankle would let her towards the narrow bridge, splashed into the water and, wincing at the coldness of the stream, crawled under the bridge. There she squatted on her hands and knees, rocks and stones slippery and hard beneath her, water soaking into her clothes, trembling both from the chill and the fear which once again gripped her.

The flowing water splashed, gurgled and bubbled around her, but she could still hear the car's engine as it approached. It grew louder and louder and then it stopped. She was almost certain it was on the bridge. Above the babbling of the stream, Lottie heard the thuds of two doors closing followed closely by voices. She couldn't make out all of the words, but she could tell that they were male and French. It must be the kidnappers! She eased herself towards the wall of the underside of the bridge, hoping against hope that the men wouldn't look under the bridge. If they did, there would be no escape. She knew she would not be able to out-run them because she would have to struggle out of the water first. Besides, her ankle still hurt. She tried to imagine what would happen.

They would see her and one would call to the other. Then they would split up, with each going to a different end of the bridge so that she could not get out without getting past at least one of them. Lottie knew that her only hope was to keep out of sight and wait and hope that they went away. The water was so cold that her hands were becoming numb. She desperately wanted to strand up, but she was terrified that if she did they would hear her and her freedom would be at an end. She waited. And she waited. The voices droned on. She could hardly make out a word, but she did hear one of the men say, "Cigarette?"

The way he said it, she could tell he must be offering a cigarette to the other. She felt a tiny hint of relief. If they were going to smoke, they might not be about to look under the bridge. They might have no idea that she was anywhere in the vicinity. She had to keep still and pray that they would finish their cigarettes and go away, but it was becoming almost impossible for her to stay still.

The cold water bit into her hands and feet. She ached from trying to hold her position and she could feel herself losing her grip on the mossy stones. She was going to slip very soon. However hard she tried, she would not be able to stay still for much longer. And then, just as she thought she could not hold on for a second longer, she saw a red glow on the water quickly followed by another. The cigarette ends floated towards her, almost touching each other, their bright red glow quickly extinguished by the chilly water. Lottie watched as the filter tips floated past her and towards the other side of the bridge. Then, above the gurgling, splashing stream, she heard a whoop of delight. "C'est a moi, j'ai gagné!" called one of the men, followed quickly by laughter from the other and words which she couldn't make out or understand. But Lottie knew what "j'ai gagné" meant: *I won!* The men had played Pooh-sticks with their cigarette ends. Just like in Winnie the Pooh, they had each tossed something into the water and then rushed to the other side of the bridge and peered over to see whose object emerged first.

Lottie wondered how they knew which cigarette butt was which, but wondered too about the strangeness of her hard-hearted kidnappers' behaviour. Could the people evil enough to seize a child and talk openly of killing her really be the same people who played Pooh-sticks like children? Lottie had just made up her mind that they couldn't and was about to try to stand up and call for help, when the car doors slammed again – thud, thud – the engine started and the vehicle chugged away into the distance.

Lottie flopped onto her side, banging her hip on a rock and soaking the last bits of her body which had remained almost dry during her ordeal. She lay in the water for a moment as she tried to summon up the energy to clamber out of the stream. She ached, she was soaked, she was tired. For a fleeting moment, she thought that it might be easier simply to give up. To lie on the stream bed and let the waters wash over

her. To fall into a sleep from which she would never wake. But then she came to her senses. She had come this far. She had battled her way through a night of fear. She had been soaked, scared and scratched. She hadn't gone through all of that only to give up and do the kidnappers' job for them. Lucky Lottie Parry was not a quitter.

Struggling, slipping and sliding, Lottie crawled from the stream and flung herself onto the bank. She slid back a little and had to grasp at reeds and nettles to prevent herself from slumping back into the water, but slowly and surely she hauled herself onto dry land where she lay panting and shivering as she tried to force herself to make her next move towards safety.

CHAPTER EIGHTEEN
PLAYING FOR

ENGLAND

Steve Parry was usually the life and soul of the England team. He was a practical joker who played tricks on his team mates and was always ready with a joke. Any new player staying in a hotel with the England team for the first time quickly learned to keep a look out for Steve.

If they left their shoes outside their rooms at night to be cleaned, they would find them replaced by ladies' shoes in the morning. Or there would be mysterious calls to their rooms from people with Italian or Spanish accents asking them if they would like to play for Milan or Real Madrid. Waiters would appear at their rooms with trays of food which they hadn't ordered – he once ordered 35 raw carrots for a new player who had asked for another spoonful at dinner!

The other players might have been annoyed at the

time, but Steve's pranks made them feel part of the team and they brought laughter and calmed their nerves before their first big matches. Steve was a popular choice as captain. The rest of the team knew he was their best player, but they also knew that he would be quick to give a word of encouragement when they made a mistake in a match, and would work his socks off for the team. England had been winning match after match since Steve became captain, and there was even talk of them winning the World Cup.

But the night before the Andorra match, the players noticed that Steve was quiet and tense. At dinner, he picked at his food and hardly ate a thing. He claimed to be tired and went to bed early, leaving his team mates to watch a film without him.

When his room mate, Richie Walker, came to bed he found Steve sitting in the dark, his head in his hands, his shoulders shaking. "What's up, Steve? Are you all right?" he asked.

He was shocked when Steve looked up. The England captain had been crying. His face was wet with tears and his brow was furrowed. "Steve, what is it?" said Richie anxiously.

"I... I... I can't tell you, mate..." he muttered, "I just can't tell you."

CHAPTER NINETEEN
CHURCH

Although the night air was cool, it was far from being cold. Yet Lottie's teeth chattered as she squelched along the road, constantly looking around her for any sign of the kidnappers. Every item of her clothing was either damp, wet or saturated. Her feet sloshed about in her trainers; her clothes clung to her; and her hair produced small rivulets of water which slid down her face and neck. She knew that she had to get out of the wet clothes and get dry, but had no idea how she might do this.

Lottie felt in her pocket for the chocolate. At least she would get some comfort from eating it. But it had gone. It must have slipped from her pocket when she was in the stream. She shuddered and tried to stifle a disappointed, frustrated sob.

Ahead of her, the first buildings of what seemed to be a small village grew as she neared them. Above them all towered the spire of the church. Might it be open? Could she shelter there? She had learned at school how people who were on the run from the law in medieval times could enter a church and claim sanctuary from

their pursuers. Once they were inside the church, they were safe from capture for forty days. Lottie didn't suppose the kidnappers would worry about entering a church to catch her, but perhaps they wouldn't even think of looking for her there.

As she entered the village, there was a sign with the word "Audrehem" on it. Lottie wondered how it was pronounced. It didn't look like a name she had ever seen before. Another oddity was the speed limit signs at either side of the road. She thought it odd that cars were allowed to travel at up to 50 miles per hour through a small village on a narrow road.

There were a few rather dim street lights which pierced the darkness and allowed her to see that the houses were mostly made of stone. None had lights on, although she was startled when passing one to find a bright light coming on from above a garage. Instinctively, Lottie ducked and crouched on the footpath with a garden wall between her and the garage. But she realised when, after a few seconds, the light went off, that it was one of those automatic devices triggered when someone moved near its sensors.

The village was silent as the population slept. No-one could see or hear the eleven-year-old girl who crept through the streets towards the church. She desperately hoped the door would be unlocked, but knew that many churches were kept locked at night to keep out vandals. Surely, she thought, no-one would come to a small village in the countryside just to damage a church. There were buildings all around the church.

Lottie was just thinking that people who lived in them would be sure to hear if anyone tried to vandalise the building, in which case perhaps it would be open, when she stopped in her tracks and stared.

There were two buildings which were larger than the nearby houses. Above the door of one she could make out a flag on a pole, drooping and still in the calm night air. But it wasn't the flag which caught her attention and startled her. It was the single word on the wall: MAIRIE. She'd seen the word before on the walls of buildings and it didn't take her long to remember where. She'd seen it in France. The Mairie was the building where the local mayor worked, and all over France the buildings displayed the tricolore, France's red, white and blue flag. Looking around carefully to ensure no-one was watching, Lottie approached the building and gazed up at the flag. Even in the gloom of the dimly lit village, she could tell that it had three colours in stripes. It wasn't a Union Jack like she'd see in England. It was almost certainly the French flag.

And then things began to fall into place. First the two cars with steering wheels on the left-hand-side; then the French voices on the bridge; the strange village name; and the speed limit signs. They weren't showing that the limit was fifty miles per hour: they were showing that it was a much slower fifty kilometres an hour. She was in France!

Before she had time to dwell on what this meant for her attempt to reach safety, Lottie's attention turned to the sounds of squeaking which seemed to be coming from near to the church. Bats! Flittering and fluttering, the small dark creatures darted and dived, their silhouettes coming in and out of view as they passed in front of street lamps. Lottie had been told that the bats you occasionally saw in England were harmless, but she wasn't so sure about those in France. She strode across the small square, almost forgetting the pain in her ankle, and made her way, fingers crossed on both hands, to the church door.

The handle was large and circular and made of cast iron. Even though she was cold and still shivering, the handle felt cold as Lottie grasped it. After looking all around for any sign of life apart from the circling bats, she pulled and then turned the handle. Nothing happened. The door remained closed. She decided to try once more, but this time, instead of pulling, she pushed as she turned. There was a creak and a clunk and then the door began to move. It wasn't locked. She was going to be able to get into the church!

As she carefully closed the heavy wooden door behind her, Lottie peered around the inside of the church. It was dark and sombre, but there was light coming from a spot about fifteen metres from where she stood. It flickered and bounced off stone pillars and wooden pews, but there was just enough for her to see the stone floor of the aisle with pews on either side, which led to the altar at the end of the church furthest from the tower. The light twinkled on a gold cross which stood on a table. Even though she was alone in a dark building, there was something comforting about the light, and the air was a little warmer than it had been outside. She made her way towards the light, her shoes still sodden and squelchy as they echoed on the stone floor.

Lottie quickly realised that the light came from a large candle which stood on a table next to several other smaller ones. She picked up one of the smaller candles and its stand, and held its wick carefully to the flame, and as it lit she began to see more of her surroundings. She listened and heard nothing, so put her candle down and picked up several of the others and lit them too. As the church became lighter near to the candle table it seemed to become darker further away, but the candles gave off a warmth, which she welcomed after her watery ordeal, and she found that she wasn't worried about the shadowy parts of the church and what might lie there.

Picking up one of the taller candles, Lottie carried it carefully as she began to explore the church. It was small and only had seats for about eighty people facing the altar and the wooden pulpit, but there were two rows of seats at right angles to the rest, near to the pulpit, and her spirits lifted as she saw what lay behind them: on each of ten pegs hung a white cotton gown. She knew she shouldn't, but Lottie was desperately tired and wet, so she set the candle on the floor and reached for one of the gowns and took it from its peg. It was a little thicker than her school blouse and she thought it would probably fit her. She needed to get out of her wet clothes. Her grandmother was always telling her and Rachel to change after they'd been out in the rain: "You'll catch your death of cold," she'd say. "You'll get pneumonia!"

Lottie had never worn such wet clothes and was surprised by how difficult it was to get them off. They seemed to stick to each other and to her, but eventually she managed and quickly slipped the gown over her head. Even though there was no-one around, she still felt embarrassed at being in church without her clothes.

The gown was long but didn't quite reach the floor, and even though her skin was still damp, she began to feel better immediately. She took down a second gown and carried it and the candle to a pew near to the candle table. On the floor between the rows of pews were firm cushions designed to be knelt upon when people were praying. Lottie needed to lie down, but the pews were too narrow. The stone floor was cold, but she drew several of the cushions together to make a bed and tested it by lying on it. It wasn't exactly comfortable, but it was better than nothing. She got up, candle in hand, and went over to the candle table where she blew out all but the large candle, leaving the church in near darkness again. Then she made her way back to the makeshift bed, rested the candle on the floor, pulled the second gown over her head and lay on the cushions. She blew out the candle and closed her eyes. At first she wriggled around as she tried to find a comfortable position but, in only a couple of minutes, tiredness overtook her and she fell into a deep sleep.

CHAPTER TWENTY
ALARM CALL

The church bells didn't wake Lottie when they began by chiming six o'clock. She slept through seven and eight o'clock too, hardly stirring but somehow incorporating the ringing into a dream about a holiday in France. The noise of tractors and cars passing the church didn't disturb her. She had missed so much sleep that she could have slept through almost anything. It was the screaming which finally woke her. Loud, piercing, shrill screaming which at first seemed to be part of a nightmare, but which gradually became reality as she stirred and opened her eyes.

She rolled over to try to find the source of the noise and this only served to increase its intensity. Then there was the sound of retreating footsteps accompanied by a panicky female voice which seemed to be saying over and over again, between shrieks, "Mon Dieu! mon Dieu! mon Dieu!

Lottie struggled to her feet. The candle had long since burnt out and daylight streamed though the coloured glass of the church windows, leaving a mosaic of colour patterning the inside of the building.

She stood blinking and wondering. It took a few moments for her to remember where she was and why, and then she began to think about the screaming. Whoever produced the screams had run away. That made a change, thought Lottie, who had spent several hours running away from people herself. As she stood on the cushions, avoiding stepping onto the cold stone floor in her bare feet, she considered what to do next.

It was morning. The sun seemed to be shining. There were people around. But she was in France. Even though she knew some French, she didn't think it would be enough to make people understand who she was and why she needed help.

And then the door creaked open and two people peered into the church warily. Lottie froze. With the light behind them, she couldn't be sure who stood at the door, but she knew that there was no way out without passing them. She took a chance. She strode towards them, suddenly and painfully recalling as she did, that she had injured her ankle. The people retreated slightly, but stayed in the doorway. It was a woman and a man. She wore a flowery dress with a blue overall and he wore a dark jacket, grey trousers and a shirt with a white collar.

"Mademoiselle?" said the man, with a little alarm in his voice as Lottie approached. "Qu'est-ce qui arrive?"

Lottie knew enough French to work out that he

had asked her what was going on. She stopped about three metres from the door and gathered her thoughts.

"Monsieur," she said, trying hard to put on a French accent, "Je suis anglaise. Je m'appelle Charlotte Parry. J'ai onze ans." Then she ran out of things she could think of to say.

The man turned to the woman and said something quietly which Lottie couldn't make out. The woman nodded and walked quickly away. The man turned back to Lottie and said, "Tu parles bien français, mademoiselle!"

"Non monsieur. Je parle français un petit peu." Lottie felt at ease with the man, even though she knew that they could only have a limited conversation. He didn't seem to speak any English and she was now struggling to think of much to say beyond asking the time and telling him which foods she liked.

They looked at each other and she began to realise how odd it must seem to find a girl asleep in a church wearing two gowns which clearly belonged to the church. She wondered if she would be in trouble, but then thought that she couldn't possibly be in as much trouble as she was when she had been kidnapped. She searched her mind for something to say.

"Je suis désolée," she said, pointing to the gown and back into the church to where she had slept. Lottie had always liked the French phrase for "I'm sorry". The man smiled. He held out his hand and gestured for Lottie to follow him out of the building. She hesitated. She was not keen to go with another stranger.

Lottie peered past the man and saw that there were people in the little village square. The woman whose screaming had woken Lottie was walking quickly towards the church with another, older, lady struggling to keep up with her. This lady wore a rather scruffy grey cardigan, which seemed far too big for her, and a long dark skirt. Lottie stepped out of the church as she approached.

"Now then, what have we here?" said the woman in a voice which sounded what her father would have called "posh". The lady spoke to the man in French and then turned to Lottie. "So you've been sleeping in the church, young lady, have you? Why on earth did you do that?"

Lottie cleared her throat. "I... er... I was trying to escape. You see... there were... there were..." and then she couldn't go on. Her shoulders heaved as the tears came. Lottie suddenly felt safe, perhaps her ordeal was finally over, but she was so full of emotion that she could hardly speak. The woman enveloped her in her arms and hugged her, stroking her hair and saying over and over, "There, there my dear, don't worry. You're safe now. No-one's going to hurt you."

After a few minutes, Lottie felt herself being led, barefoot, still with the woman's arm around her shoulders, across the square. The sun had been hidden by clouds and it looked as if rain might be imminent. "Now what you need is a nice hot drink and something to eat, then you can tell me all about it. The priest here, Father Jean, he'll telephone the police and we'll soon have you back with your family." She paused just as they reached the door of a stone cottage. "You do have a family don't you my dear?"

Between sobs, Lottie said that she did and that she wanted her mum and dad. "Of course you do, my dear. And we'll soon find them for you, I promise. What's your name? I'm Ruth Barlow, by the way, and this is Madame Berteaux." And she led Lottie into the cottage, accompanied by the lady who had found her in the church.

Lottie looked around her. There were paintings everywhere: some hung on the walls, but most leaned against walls or were propped against various old, wooden chests and cupboards. There were two leaning against the backs of armchairs, and Lottie struggled to find somewhere to sit when the lady invited her to do so. The room was untidy and rather disorganised, with paint brushes and tubes of paint covering almost every surface. The pictures were striking. They were mostly landscapes, large and bold with bright colours. There were seascapes in brilliant blues, and sunsets with reds, oranges and yellows casting bright light onto darkening hills and fields. "What do you think?" asked the woman. "Load of old rubbish the lot, but I do my best!"

Lottie gazed around at dozens of canvases. "They're wonderful. They're so... so warm and inviting."

"My word, I think we've found an art critic!" said the woman, turning to the other lady. "Extra croissants for you, I think!" And with that, she went out of the room and quickly returned bearing plates of croissants, fruit and cheese. There was jam and butter, and the lady swept paints and brushes from a coffee table to make room to put them down. Soon the food was joined by orange juice and hot chocolate. Lottie drank deeply from a large cup, burning her lips and tongue slightly, but hugely enjoying the feeling of drinking something hot and comforting.

She tried to remember her manners, but ate greedily from the plate of warm croissants. When she tried to pick up the crumbs which fell from her mouth, the woman told her not to worry. "It's not exactly Buckingham Palace my dear, I'll sweep up later. A bit more mess isn't going to make much difference!"

When she finally began to feel a little full, Lottie paused from her breakfast and spoke to the two women, "Thank you very much," she said. "I'm really sorry about the church and the gowns. I was lost and frightened and I had to find somewhere to hide."

Ruth Barlow turned to the French lady and spoke a few words to explain what Lottie had said. The Frenchwoman looked concerned and asked a question which Ruth translated. "You said you were frightened. Why was that? Are you in some kind of danger?"

Lottie cleared her throat. She hadn't spoken to anyone since the previous night and she'd been unable to tell anyone about the kidnap. Now she wondered what to say. How could she tell these strangers about the ordeal she had been through? Wouldn't it sound like a fantasy? When she finally plucked up the courage to speak, her words spilled out rapidly as if she was frightened that pausing for breath would make her break down and cry again.

"There was a woman in England... and I got into her car because I thought she was my Mum's friend, but she wasn't, and then I woke up and I was in a farmhouse, and there were two men, and I was tied up, and they said they'd kill me if my Dad didn't let Andorra score twice, and I escaped and hid, and then I found out I was in France..." She stopped. The women were staring at her, one of them unsure what Lottie had been saying, the other studying her as if to try to work out if she was telling the truth.

"I'm sorry," said Lottie, "you must think I'm mad. You probably think I'm making all this up, but I'm not, honestly."

Ruth Barlow spoke gently. "We don't think you're mad, my dear... by the way, what is your name?"

"Lottie... Charlotte... Charlotte Parry."

"Well Charlotte Parry, or shall we call you Lottie?

You are safe now. The priest will get the police and we can telephone your parents and tell them where you are."

Lottie began to cry, but managed to say, "Please call me Lottie. I'm so sorry to eat all your croissants and take up your time, but please could we phone my mum and dad now."

"Of course we can, my dear. I'm afraid I don't have a telephone, let alone one of those dreadful mobile things, but we can go across to Father Jean's house and use his. But first you need some clothes. Madame Berteaux has put those wet things you left in the church into the washing machine, and they won't be dry for ages, and as you can see, my things would be far too big for you." She said a few words to Madame Berteaux, who smiled and left the house.

"She's going to fetch you some of her daughter's old clothes. She's a bit bigger than you, but I'm sure you'd rather wear her things than the choir robes! Why don't you make use of the bathroom while she's gone. You can have a shower and I'll find you a spare toothbrush.

So Lottie allowed herself to be led from the chaotic living room to a staircase with pictures hanging close together from the walls. A large grandfather clock on the landing half way up the stairs told her it was 10.30 – there was plenty of time to contact her father before the match.

Upstairs she was surprised to find a bathroom which was clean, tidy and modern. Ruth Barlow could see she was taken aback to find such a contrast from the rest of the house. "I bet you expected the same mess in here as in the living room, didn't you Lottie? Well I like to keep a couple of rooms free from that junk I paint. It's nice to be able to sit in the bath or lie on the bed without having to look at a picture and start to find all its faults."

"But I think your pictures are lovely," said Lottie, and she meant it. "I wish I could paint like that."

"You're too kind, Lottie. Still, fortunately some other people do seem to like them. I manage to sell enough to keep me in France for half of the year. It's hard to believe anyone would spend five hundred Euros on one of my pictures, but some people clearly have more money than sense!"

With that, she found a towel and an old blue dressing gown, a new toothbrush and fresh soap, and told Lottie to help herself to shampoo. "You take your time, Lottie. My bedroom's across the corridor. I'll put the clothes in there and when you're dressed you can come down and we'll go and make that telephone call."

Lottie closed the bathroom door behind her, leaned against the door and heaved a deep sigh of relief. It was all going to be all right. Soon, she'd be clean and have dry clothes on. She'd speak to her parents and tell her father that she was safe and that the only goals he needed to score were *for* England. In a few hours she'd probably be back on the other side of the Channel and heading for home. It was almost certainly too late to get to Wembley for the match, but she'd watch on television later and she'd be so proud when her father led his team onto the pitch. But even though she was happier than she'd been for several hours, Lottie still shook as she sobbed with relief.

CHAPTER TWENTY-ONE
VISITORS

The news of an eleven-year-old girl being found in the church dressed in choir gowns spread through the tiny village like wildfire. Soon there were around twenty people gathered in the square sharing what they had heard. Some said that the girl was a refugee who had escaped from a camp at Calais, while others said that she was running away from the police because she had broken into a house. The rumours grew as people met and talked.

When Madame Berteaux walked across the square towards Ruth Barlow's cottage holding a pile of girls' clothes in front of her, people converged upon her to seek information. They asked about thieves and refugees, but all she would tell them was that there was a little girl who had lost her parents and that they were looking after her until the police came, and that Father Jean had called the police but had been told that, as there was no emergency, they would not be able to come until they had finished dealing with a traffic accident near Nordausque.

After that, many people turned their conversation

to the road accident, some worrying about friends and relatives who might have been travelling in the area, others bemoaning the driving standards of their fellow countrymen. Some people noticed the blue Volvo which parked near the church, but most were too preoccupied with their speculations about crashes and the lost girl. Those who did notice thought the two men and the woman who got out of the car seemed ordinary enough, although they were wearing sunglasses and hats, which seemed a little odd on an overcast morning. They were probably tourists on their way somewhere who had stopped to admire the medieval church or look for a café or a boulangerie. The people were friendly enough, pausing to chat to the villagers, enquiring about the reason so many were gathered in the square, and seeming genuinely concerned when they heard about the girl who had lost her parents. They asked what the girl looked like and were given a range of descriptions, mostly from people who had not actually seen her but had heard about her from others. The one thing that most agreed upon was that the girl had dark skin and was about eleven or twelve years old. The two men and the woman seemed very interested when they heard that, and were especially eager to find out if the police had been called. When they heard about the delay they acted quickly.

CHAPTER TWENTY-TWO
A REUNION

Lottie had emerged from the shower feeling warm and refreshed. The soft fluffy towel was large enough to wrap around her from shoulders to ankles, and she hugged it to herself and put the old blue dressing gown on top. Then she made her way to Ruth Barlow's bedroom, where she found a neat pile of clothes on the bed with an ancient hair dryer and hair brush sitting on top. The plug on the hair dryer wasn't like the ones she was used to in England, but she quickly worked out how to plug it into a socket by the bed and sat brushing her curly hair with one hand, while she moved the rather noisy dryer back and forth with the other. It wasn't like the hairdryers she'd used at home and in hotels. There was no safety switch, so once it was going you didn't have to keep a finger on the switch to keep it working

She looked down at the clothes. There was a pair of denim jeans which looked fine, but were not exactly the latest fashion. A cream woollen jumper seemed more promising and there was a white tee shirt, knickers and socks, all spotlessly clean and ironed. Her mother never ironed underwear or socks, and it seemed strange to see items which no-one was going to see looking so neat. Next to the pile was a pair of sandals, which looked as if they would probably be a little too large for her and certainly didn't look like the kind of footwear she would have chosen for herself.

Lottie jumped when she saw the bedroom door open. She hadn't heard footsteps on the creaky stairs because of the hairdryer. Ruth Barlow put her head round the door and held a finger to her lips. She closed the door behind her and gently took the hair dryer from Lottie and placed it, still running, on the bed. Then she gestured for Lottie to come to her.

"Lottie, there are people downstairs who say they are your mother and your uncle."

Lottie's face lit up. "My Mum, she's here? Brilliant!" and she made to leave the room. Ruth held onto her and stopped her from reaching the door.

"Wait, Lottie! I'm not sure it is your Mum. And the man who says he's your uncle, he's French. Do you have a French uncle, Lottie?"

Lottie shook her head.

"They say you ran away from them after an argument and that they've come to take you home. Is that true, Lottie?"

Lottie shook her head again. Once again, she was gripped by fear. In the pit of her stomach she felt a small pain as she contemplated being taken away by the kidnappers again. She knew they had guns and they would probably use them if anyone tried to prevent them from taking her. She had put Ruth Barlow and Madame Berteaux in danger, and they had been so kind to her.

Ruth picked up the clothes and gestured for Lottie to follow her. "We'll leave the hairdryer running so they think you're still here," she said. Then she led Lottie to the narrow corridor and turned right, away from the stairs. Looking around carefully to check that no-one had come upstairs, Ruth led Lottie to another room. Downstairs they could hear people's voices, but not the words they spoke. The hairdryer droned in the background as Ruth opened a low wooden door and they crept into a room with drawn curtains. Even in the gloom, Lottie could see that the room was filled with paintings, easels, paints and brushes. "My studio!" whispered Ruth, and, closing the door behind them, mouthed and mimed, "Get dressed, quickly!"

Lottie stared for a moment and then Ruth turned her back while Lottie hurried out of the dressing gown and towel, still a little damp from her shower, and put on the clothes Madame Berteaux had brought, as quickly as she could. When she was ready, Ruth pointed to a hatch in the ceiling. "It's a loft," she whispered. "If you can climb up there and hide, I'll open the bathroom window and make it look as if you've run away."

Lottie was about to say that she had tried that trick once before, when there was a loud creak from the stairs followed by a voice calling, "Madame, la maman, elle demande voir sa fille." It was Madame Berteaux. The kidnappers were clearly becoming tired of waiting to recapture their prey.

CHAPTER TWENTY-THREE

THE LOFT

Ruth Barlow snatched a pile of canvases from a wooden chair and placed it under the hatch in the low ceiling. "Quick Lottie," she said, holding the chair and urging the girl to climb onto it. Lottie did as she was told and, once on the chair, pushed against the wooden hatch until it tipped backwards with a thud.

"Oh my God, they'll hear!" said Ruth, but Lottie hauled herself up from the chair and into the loft. "If you crawl along that way," said Ruth indicating with her hand, "you'll be able to hide behind some boxes. Stay on the wooden beams. If you put your foot on the plaster, you'll come through the ceiling! Quick, close the hatch behind you!"

And with that, Ruth and Lottie gave nervous waves to each other and parted, Lottie into the dark, cobwebby loft with its sloping ceiling and small dusty packing cases; Ruth to the kidnappers who waited impatiently in her living room.

The loft was not quite dark. Narrow shafts of light penetrated through gaps between the tiles and dust seemed to hover in the air in the brightness. Lottie knelt uncomfortably on a roof beam, thankful that the jeans protected her knees more than her shorts would have done. There were boxes everywhere, piled on top of each other in the centre of the loft where the roof was highest. At the edges there were single boxes and piles of canvases. Lottie could tell that the boxes rested on the wooden beams. The plaster which lay between the beams and formed the ceiling of the rooms below would have been too weak to take their weight.

The air was still and warm. Yet again, Lottie could feel her heart pounding. Only a few metres below her lay extreme danger. Down in the living room the kidnappers were losing patience. It would not be long before they came up the stairs to look for her. If they didn't believe she had escaped through the bathroom window, it would only be a matter of time before they explored further and entered the loft. She knew she was trapped. There was nowhere to run. She could hide behind the boxes, but that would mean trying to move about in the loft and she would risk making a noise or even putting her foot through the flimsy plaster.

As she waited, a thousand thoughts flashed through Lottie's mind. She thought of the people who mattered most in her life: her mother and father, her sister, her best friend Ellie, her grandparents. She wished she'd never argued with her sister. Now she thought she might never see Rachel again, she promised herself that if she did she'd never fall out with her again. And she'd tidy her room when she was told to, and she'd...

Lottie froze. Suddenly there were voices beneath her. Angry voices. "We are not asking again, Madame. We want the child now!" Instinctively, Lottie looked down in the direction the voices came from. There was a chink of light from the plaster. She squatted as low as she could and tried to peer through the tiny hole.

There was another voice. It was the woman. "Look, there's a loft. Is that where she's hiding? Tell us, now! My friend here is not afraid to use that gun. Just give us the girl and you won't get hurt."

Through the small gap, Lottie could make out the tops of the heads of the two kidnappers. She heard Ruth Barlow's voice. "Of course she's not in the loft. How could she possibly get up there? I've told you, she must have climbed out of the bathroom window when she heard your voices. She's a plucky girl that Lottie, and she's clever: far too clever for a pair of dim-witted thugs like you two!"

There was a sudden crack, followed by a muffled "Owww!" They had slapped Ruth. "How dare they?" thought Lottie, anger rising in her like mercury in a thermometer in a sudden heat wave. She was furious. This lady had helped her, fed her, found her clothes and let her get clean and dry. She didn't deserve to be hit by these cowards.

A strange feeling came over Lottie. She didn't weigh up advantages and disadvantages as she had before. She didn't really think at all. She simply stood up with her feet on the roof beams and jumped. She felt the ceiling give way as she descended. She banged her arm on a beam, and then she connected very hard with the heads and shoulders of the two kidnappers. Her landing was painful, but nowhere near as painful as it was for the crooks.

A gun flew from the man's hand and hit a wall and began to spin on the floorboards. Ruth Barlow swooped and grabbed it before the kidnapper had chance to recover. She held it in both hands, pointing it steadily at the villains. She pulled back the trigger until it clicked and spoke with a calmness that Lottie thought she could not possibly feel. "Don't move, either of you! I know exactly how to use this gun and if you even breathe too loudly, I will show you why I have a cupboard full of trophies for marksmanship."

Lottie had picked herself up and obediently followed Ruth's instruction to move away from the kidnappers and stand behind her. "I want you to go downstairs now, Lottie, and ask Madame Berteaux to fetch Father Jean. Go quickly now. If either of these two good-for-nothings moves, I'll shoot them, and you're far too young to have to witness something like that." The man and woman lay on the floor, shattered pieces of plasterboard clinging to their clothing. The

man began to speak, but before he managed any more than "Madame..." Ruth interrupted him, "Shut up!" she snapped. "One word, one movement, and I will rid the world of your miserable presence. Spread your arms and legs out and keep still!" Groaning and muttering, the man and woman did as they were told.

Lottie was filled with admiration for her host's courage and was about to go downstairs when a dreadful thought came to her. There was another man! Where was he? He probably had a gun too. How long would he wait before he came into the house? He'd know something was wrong. He'd probably come up the stairs and find his friends held at gunpoint. What would he do then? There could be shooting. Someone might be killed.

As the kidnappers lay on the floor, Lottie saw their eyes meet. She could tell they were planning something.

"I need to look out of the window," said Lottie, and she gave the kidnappers a wide berth as she moved across the room and peered through the narrow gap between the curtains. Outside, across the square, the blue Volvo was still parked, but there was no-one sitting in it and no sign of the other man.

Then she saw him. He was talking to two women in the square near to the cottage. Lottie knew it would not be long before he came to the front door. She prayed that the police would arrive soon, but didn't think it was likely. She needed to get a message to Father Jean, but didn't dare leave the house while the man was outside. She couldn't think of the words to say to Madame Berteaux to get her to urge the priest to come.

Lottie could tell Ruth Barlow was nervous, despite her brave and menacing words to the crooks. She didn't want to mention the other man in case she frightened her, but she had to do something quickly. The spread-eagled kidnappers caught each other's eyes again and Lottie was sure she saw the man nod his head very slightly. He was only a metre from where she stood near the window He was going to try to grab her. Lottie knew it a split second before he made his move, and she instinctively jumped as his arm shot towards her leg. Then everything happened at once. The woman tried to get up, the man grasped at thin air, and Lottie landed with both feet firmly on his outstretched arm. A deafening shot rang out and Ruth shouted with the fiercest voice Lottie had ever heard. "The next one'll blow your brains out!"

Lottie backed away to the furthest corner of the room, as the man cursed and swore in agony as he clutched his broken arm. There was a splintered hole in the floor boards next to him where the bullet had struck.

Lottie's ears rang from the explosive sound of the gunfire. The kidnappers lay still, but the man continued to whimper with pain. But his moans were quickly drowned out by the clatter of footsteps coming up the stairs.

CHAPTER TWENTY-FOUR
STALEMATE

"Madame Barlow! Madame Barlow! Qu'est-ce qui arrive?" Madame Berteaux's anxious voice was suddenly muffled and there was the sound of a struggle from the landing. Then silence. Or almost silence. The hairdryer droned on in the next room and then there were anxious sounds of "Mmmm... mmm", followed by the voice of the third kidnapper.

"I'm coming in the room. I have the woman and I will shoot her if I have to!"

And then the door burst open and in came Madame Berteaux, the man's arm around her neck, his gun pointed at her head. "Levez-vous!" he said to his colleagues, who began to get up from the floor, the man clutching his broken arm and wincing.

"Stop!" yelled Ruth, pointing her gun steadily at the half-sitting kidnappers. "And you," she shouted, gesturing towards the third kidnapper, who continued to hold Madame Berteaux and point his gun at her head, "Put your gun down and let my friend go or I'll blast you to kingdom come!"

"Oh no, madame," responded the gunman, "it is

you who must put down the gun. Do it now and your friend I will let go! We'll take the girl and you will not see us again."

Madame Berteaux's face was contorted with fear, but she managed to shake her head as she looked at Ruth. "I think my friend is trying to tell me that she doesn't want you to let her go if it means that Lottie goes with you."

Lottie could tell that the man was unsure of what to do next. He looked from Ruth to his friends, who were still half-sitting and half lying on the floor. Ruth seemed amazingly calm, but Lottie's stomach churned as she wondered what would happen next.

"I think what we have, Monsieur, is a stand off, a stalemate," said Ruth with a firm, clear voice. "You could shoot Madame Berteaux, I suppose, but I would certainly shoot you and probably both of your friends if you did. Or I might just decide to shoot you all anyway. Come and stand behind me Lottie. If he does manage to fire back I don't want him to hit you."

Lottie could hardly believe what Ruth Barlow was saying. She seemed to be taking control of the situation and she seemed incredibly confident and self-assured.

Ruth spoke again. "Now I think you have just one real option," she said, staring hard at the man with the gun. You can let Madame Berteaux go, put down your gun and get out of my house. You might just manage it before the police get here, and I'm sure that now people have heard the shot I fired, they will be here very soon indeed." The kidnappers exchanged glances. Lottie could tell they were trying to make a decision.

"Make your minds up quickly," said Ruth. "I'm going to count to five and then I'll make them up for you! One... two..."

The woman spoke, "But if Claude puts his gun down you might shoot him anyway," she said anxiously.

"Three... that's a chance you'll have to take, isn't it... four..."

And then, almost miraculously, the villains made their decision. The man released Madame Berteaux and pushed her away from him. The others got up from the floor gingerly and moved towards the door and followed the gunman's instruction to leave the room. When they had passed him he lowered the gun to the floor and quickly left the room, shutting the door behind him. There was a clatter of footsteps on the stairs followed quickly by the slamming of a door. Ruth moved to the window and drew back the curtains just in time to hear the sirens from approaching police cars. Moments later, three cars screeched to a halt in the village square and a dozen police spilled out. Lottie saw the kidnappers stop and look around frantically as they were surrounded. Then the police barked orders at them and they lay prostrate on the cobbles before being searched for weapons, handcuffed and led away to the cars. Lottie saw four policeman approach the front door of the house, guns held at the ready, and then she heard a crash.

She jerked her head round to find Ruth Barlow lying on the floor, the gun still in her hand, with Madame Berteaux leaning earnestly over her, weeping. Then there was a piercing "No-o-o-n!" from the Frenchwoman as she watched Lottie collapse to the floor too.

CHAPTER TWENTY-FIVE

MEMORIES

The first thing Lottie saw when she came to was a bright strip of light. It took her a few seconds to work out that it was a fluorescent tube. Then she realised that she could only see out of her right eye. There was something covering her left. And her left arm wouldn't move. She tried to move her legs, but her right leg seemed to be stuck.

Thoughts flooded through her mind. Where was she? Why couldn't she move properly? She seemed to be in bed, but this wasn't her bed. Whose bed was it? And then she recalled another occasion when she'd been on a bed unable to move properly. There had been a woman and two men. They had wanted to talk to her father. Why was that? Who were they?

And then she remembered something else: a lady: a lady with a gun, but not the bad lady. A lady who had tried to help her. But something awful had happened. There had been a scream. The lady had been on the floor and another lady was screaming. And then everything was blank.

There had been guns and police. Had the lady been

shot? Had she been shot herself? Was that why she couldn't move her arm and leg? There had been bad people. They had tied her up. Had they captured her again?

Her head hurt. The recollection and speculation made it hurt more. Her mouth was dry. Her throat was sore. She realised that she needed a drink. Water: that's what she needed. She remembered water. There had been a ditch and rats. And there had been a stream and a bridge. She had been cold; really cold, and wet, and frightened; really frightened. Should she still be afraid? Where was she? Why wasn't anyone there? She tried to call out, but her dry mouth and sore throat wouldn't let her. Her lips were sore. She felt the dry skin with her tongue. It seemed as if she'd been eating something salty or as if she'd swallowed seawater. And then the effort of remembering and trying to call out became too much for her and she slipped back into unconsciousness.

CHAPTER TWENTY-SIX
RUTH BARLOW

"Lotteee... Lotteee... ah, ma petite, you are awaking."

Lottie's uncovered eye blinked rapidly as she stirred herself back into consciousness. The light was bright and it made her squint, but she made out, leaning over her, a pretty, dark-haired young woman; a nurse.

"Lotteee... Lotteee..." Why did this woman say that word in such a strange way? And then she remembered. That was her name, Lottie, and she had been in France. Was she still in France? She tried to speak, but struggled to shape her dry mouth to make the words come out.

"Ah Lotteee, you would like some water, yes?" The nurse had a gentle, melodious voice. When she spoke, it was almost as if she was singing. Lottie watched as the nurse lifted a plastic cup to her lips. It was the kind of cup Rachel used to use when she was a baby. It had a lid in it and a sort of spout to drink from. She wondered why she was being given a drink from a baby's cup. She didn't think she was a baby. But then nothing seemed to be as it should be. Perhaps she had travelled back in time.

The water tasted wonderful. Never could she

remember a drink being so welcome. She enjoyed the feel of the water in her mouth and as it slipped down her throat. It was like a magic potion. It made her feel almost instantly better. She was sorry when the nurse took the cup away from her lips.

She made another attempt to speak and this time the words came out. "Where am I?" The voice she heard didn't sound like what she thought was her normal voice, but the nurse seemed to understand.

"Ah Lotteee, you are in the hospital, but you are going to be all right. The doctor is telling me that you have, how do you say, a break of the arm. And yes, you have hurt your ankle too, but he is not thinking that it is breaking too. And you have a bump of the head, but it is going to be better too."

"I'm in France aren't I?"

"But yes, naturally ma petite. But don't worry, you will be able to go home very soon."

A huge wave of relief swelled through Lottie's body at the thought of home. She was safe. She hadn't been kidnapped again. She was alive. She'd be able to see her sister, mother and father again. Her father? She remembered her father. There was something he had to do. Something he didn't want to do. And then it came to her – football, England, Andorra, goals.

"I need to speak to my dad, please, I need to speak to him right now! What time is it?"

"Now cherie, don't be agitated. You will see your

father soon. But it is only two thirty and he will be playing football now."

"But that's why I need to talk to him!" insisted Lottie. "I need to speak to him before the match starts."

"But it has already started, Lottee. In France is one hour forward of England. Here it is two thirty; in England it is three thirty."

"No-o-o-o!" cried Lottie. "N-o-o-o!" but the nurse stroked her forehead and spoke gently. "There, there, ma petite. Do not worry. He will be here later this evening to tell you all about the football match. Anyway, I have someone here who wants to see you. Would you like a visitor, cherie?"

And then there was someone else in the room. There was a familiar voice: a "posh" voice; a voice Lottie didn't think she would ever hear again. "Now then Lottie, old girl, how are you? You've been in the wars I think, and I gather it's all my fault!"

"Ruth," said Lottie softly, a tear rolling down her cheek. "You're alive! I... I thought they'd shot you."

"Nothing of the sort, my dear. I'm afraid I rather let the side down and fainted. Must have been with relief after seeing those crooks off the premises!"

Memories were flooding back now. Lottie remembered how she had hurt her arm. "I'm sorry about your ceiling," she said.

"Good heavens, Lottie! If you hadn't jumped through my ceiling I might be in the mortuary now. You saved my life. You're a proper hero, or is it heroine? I'm never quite sure. Anyway, you were tremendously brave and I gather you broke your arm in the process."

Lottie raised her head from the pillow and looked at her arm. It was in plaster and was raised above the bed by a sort of cord attached to a stand. She thought her arm ought to hurt, but she couldn't feel any pain, although she did begin to notice some discomfort from her ankle. Then she thought about her father again.

"We've got to get a message to my father. He might not have let Andorra score yet."

"Ah yes, the football match," said Ruth, "I'm afraid it's a bit too late to do anything about that now. I can't believe the lengths those crooks went to just to get Andorra to score two goals."

"But my father will hate doing that, we've got to try and stop him," pleaded Lottie. "Can't we phone him, or Wembley Stadium or the police?"

"I don't think that would be a good idea, Lottie. You couldn't ring your father because he's in the middle of a match, and I really don't think he'd want anyone to know if he had deliberately let the other team score two goals. People might not understand and he could end up in a lot of trouble. Can you imagine the headlines: 'International footballer deliberately gives goals to the opposition'. I think we'd better leave things to your dad to sort out. From what I hear, he's a brilliant player. I'm sure that if he gives Andorra two goals, he'll make sure that England score three!"

Lottie wasn't convinced, but tiredness overcame her and she fell into a troubled sleep.

CHAPTER TWENTY-SEVEN
A RECORD

Lottie would never forget the look on Ruth Barlow's face when she told her. She had burst into Lottie's hospital room with the broadest of grins on her face and a piece of paper in her hand. "I've just been watching the football results on the television in the waiting room, Lottie. I wrote one of them down because I thought you might like to see it."

Ruth handed Lottie the scrap of paper. Printed neatly in blue biro, the words swam in front of Lottie's eyes. She had to squint through tears of joy as she read them:

ENGLAND 14 (FOURTEEN) ANDORRA 2
ENGLAND GOALSCORERS: PARRY 8, ROONEY 3, STERLING, SHAW AND WELBECK
ANDORRA GOALSCORERS: PARRY (2 OWN GOALS)

"I don't really know all that much about football, I'm afraid, Lottie, but I think that's rather a big score, isn't it?"

Lottie nodded.

Ruth went on, "The French sports presenter was very excited. Apparently, it's the biggest score England have ever had and your Dad has broken the England record for the most goals by one player. And I mean the eight he scored for England, not the two he scored against them."

"But won't he get into trouble for scoring the own goals?" asked Lottie.

"I don't think so my dear. I gather he'd already scored six for England when he "accidentally" put the ball past his own goalkeeper twice in five minutes. The presenter said it was the goalkeeper's fault both times, but I think we know differently, don't we? I'm absolutely certain he won't get into any trouble. People will be too busy talking about the eight goals he scored for England. There was a reporter on the programme who said he had never seen a player so determined to score goals."

Through her tears and gulping sobs, Lottie managed to get out the words, "He did that for me... he did that to save me... and he still showed everyone that he's the best player..." And then Lottie was convulsed with sobbing. She wanted to roll over and bury her head in the pillow, but with her arm and leg held in place she could only lie there crying and crying while Ruth tried to comfort her. She cried with relief that she was safe and with joy that Ruth was too, and she cried because her father, her wonderful father, had risked his career to make sure his daughter was safe. And he'd still managed to be a "national treasure" as he did so!

CHAPTER TWENTY-EIGHT
A HOLIDAY

There were red, white and blue balloons tied to the sign at the edge of Audrehem when Becky drove into the little village. Steve, Lottie and Rachel pointed to them and then to the Union Jacks which fluttered from lamp posts and buildings. Someone very special was going to visit the village and the little square was crowded with men, women and children who all dutifully stood to one side as Becky drove the car slowly towards Ruth Barlow's cottage.

Before she could get there, Becky brought the car to a halt. "I daren't go any further in case I knock someone over. I think we'll have to walk from here."

"Ruth must have told them you were coming, Dad," said Lottie, who was used to seeing her famous father being greeted by crowds, especially since he scored ten goals in a match. Steve turned to his daughter, smiled and winked. "Aye, maybe," he said. "Come on, let's see if we can battle our way to Mrs Barlow's door. And with that, he and Becky climbed out of the car. Lottie and Rachel pushed the buttons on the doors to lower the electric windows, but they couldn't

get out until their parents opened the doors because of the child locks. People were standing close to the car, but no-one pressed up against it like they did in England if they saw Steve at a petrol station or at traffic lights. Sometimes it was quite frightening when people seemed to want to get into the car to talk to the England captain.

There was a cheer when the crowd saw Steve and everyone clapped, but this was nothing compared to the roar which went up, followed by thunderous applause, when Lottie finally got out of the car. A band struck up and played "God save the Queen", and the crowd parted so that Lottie and her family could walk the rest of the way across the square to Ruth's house. Lottie smiled nervously as people held out their hands to shake hers, and she saw people holding banners and placards with the words "Allez Lottie!" and "Bienvenue Lottie".

And as she stood gazing in amazement at dozens of smiling French people, all of whom seemed delighted to see her, Lottie looked around at the Mairie, which sported the red and white flag of St George alongside the French tricolore. She gazed at the church and remembered the dark night six weeks earlier when she had been startled by bats and had crept into the church to find shelter. Above the crowd, she could see the roof of Ruth Barlow's cottage, and she recalled her dramatic descent from the loft onto the heads of the crooks below. Ruth had sent her copies of the French papers and Becky had translated them for the family. Lottie knew that she'd been described as a hero by the French press, but she had never expected the greeting the villagers were now giving her.

Then there was a lot of shushing and whispering and the people fell silent. From the crowd stepped a smiling and rather dignified man, dressed in robes and wearing medals on his chest. He coughed slightly to clear his throat and then made a short speech, most of which Lottie didn't understand, but when it ended he kissed her on both cheeks and shook her hand, before handing her a small box which he gestured for her to open. Lottie looked at her parents, who nodded and smiled, and then she removed the lid to find a silver medal the size of a two pound coin, held on a red, white and blue ribbon. On one side was a coat of arms and on the other the words: "In honour of Charlotte Parry: an English heroine". As she stared at the medal, Lottie felt her mother's hand on her shoulder and she knew what she needed to do. She too cleared her throat and said, "Merci Monsieur, Merci beaucoup, Monsieur!"

There was more cheering and then more shushing, and Lottie looked up from admiring her medal to see the smiling, kindly face of Ruth Barlow, with an equally happy looking Madame Berteaux standing behind her. "I see you've met Monsieur le Maire, Lottie. Welcome to Audrehem once again. I'm glad it's in happier circumstances this time!"

Before Ruth could say any more or even hug and kiss Steve, Becky and Rachel, the mayor cleared his throat again and made another short speech, before presenting Ruth with a medal too. Ruth was clearly rather surprised by this, but managed to make a polite speech back in French, during which she frequently pointed to Lottie and used her name. Once again, the crowd cheered an applauded and many called out "à bientôt, à bientôt, Lottie," as Ruth led the Parry family to her cottage. "They're all looking forward to seeing you at the village hall tonight, Lottie, said Ruth. Apparently, they're giving a party in your honour!"

And as they entered the little cottage, which Lottie noticed was considerably tidier than last time she had visited, Rachel squeezed Lottie's hand and her parents each put an arm around her shoulders. "It was bad enough having a national treasure in the family," said Becky, her face glowing with pride, "now we've got to put up with an international treasure as well. I don't know how we'll manage, do you, Rachel?"